What We Saw

More from MARY DOWNING HAHN

The Thirteenth Cat

The Puppet's Payback and Other Chilling Tales

Guest

The Girl in the Locked Room

One for Sorrow

Took

Where I Belong

Mister Death's Blue-Eyed Girls

The Doll in the Garden

Closed for the Season

The Ghost of Crutchfield Hall

Deep and Dark and Dangerous

Witch Catcher

The Old Willis Place

Hear the Wind Blow

Anna on the Farm

Promises to the Dead

Anna All Year Round

As Ever, Gordy

Following My Own Footsteps

The Gentleman Outlaw and Me—Eli

Look for Me by Moonlight

Time for Andrew

The Wind Blows Backward

Stepping on the Cracks

The Spanish Kidnapping Disaster

The Dead Man in Indian Creek

December Stillness

Following the Mystery Man

Tallahassee Higgins

Wait Till Helen Comes

The Jellyfish Season

Daphne's Book

The Time of the Witch

The Sara Summer

ING HAHN

WHAT WE SAW

a thriller

Clarion Books
An Imprint of HarperCollins*Publishers*

Clarion Books is an imprint of HarperCollins Publishers.

ISBN 978-0-35-841441-4

Typography by Jenna Stempel-Lobell
22 23 24 25 26 PC/LSCC 10 9 8 7 6 5 4 3 2 1
❖
First Edition

For Ann

In memory of our tree house,
of the mysteries we hoped to solve,
of bicycles and roller skates
and swimming pools,
of books and paper dolls
and dollhouses,
of woods and trees
and creeks and railroad tracks,
of all the things our mothers didn't know
but didn't matter
as long as we were home in time for dinner.

1

For some reason, boredom maybe, Skylar picks the hottest day of the summer to ride our bikes all the way to the town limits.

I ask her why, and she says, "Don't you want to see exactly where Evansburg stops and Newton starts? Haven't you ever wondered about endings and beginnings?"

"Not really," I say. "I'd rather talk your mother into driving us to the pool."

"I'm not in the mood for swimming. I want to do something different."

"Like have heatstroke and go to the hospital?"

"Oh, come on, Abbi. School starts in a few weeks. Let's go somewhere we've never been. Aren't you tired of doing the same old boring thing day after day? Pool, mall, library. Pool, mall, library."

I try to reason with her. "In case you forgot, that side of town is where that girl we call Slap Your Face lives. What if we see her and she starts calling us names like she does in school? Or she slaps us like she slapped Lindsey?"

"She must be in juvie by now," Skylar says. "I know for a fact she shoplifts at the mall."

"How about Jason and Carter? They live over there too."

Skylar shrugs. "They're probably in the state pen."

"I wish."

"We'll take some pictures and go home, Abbi. We won't be there long enough to see anybody we know."

Even though I think it's a dumb thing to do, I run out of arguments and end up letting her talk me into a long, hot bike ride to a place I don't want to go.

We take Grant Road to Route 203 and ride along the shoulder. Traffic roars past close enough to touch. The sun beats down on us. The smell of diesel fumes chokes me. I'm scared I'll fall off my bike and an eighteen-wheeler will run me over.

We turn off the highway and take the road to Newton. Skylar coasts to a stop and checks the mileage on her bike. "We've only ridden five miles," she says. "That's hardly any distance."

"If you added extra for the hills, it would be twenty

miles," I say. "And if you factored in the temperature, it would be fifty miles."

Skylar pushes her hair out of her face. We're growing our hair long this summer. So far, hers has grown faster than mine. It touches her shoulders already, a blond mane of thick waves. Mine is wispy and as fine as a baby's, hanging around my face in a tangle of red curls. No matter how long it gets, it won't look like Skylar's hair.

I'll never look like Skylar either. She's an inch taller than me, wears a bra, and is the prettiest girl in our class. She's my best friend, so I try not to be jealous. Mom says, "Just wait till you're eighteen. By then you'll be beautiful."

It's a long time to wait. Why can't I be just a little pretty now?

At least Skylar's not smarter than I am. We both pull down easy As in most of our classes. She gets ahead in math sometimes but never in language arts. Her main talent is singing, and mine is art. I can't sing, and she can't draw, so we're even there.

I have one advantage, though. I'll be thirteen three months before Skylar, so I'll be a teenager first. Which isn't much of a consolation, but still, I plan to remind her that I'm older than she is as frequently as possible.

Skylar interrupts my thoughts. "There's a gas station across the street. Let's get water."

It's the first sensible thing she's said all day. I fish around in my pockets to find what's left of my allowance—one damp, wrinkled dollar bill. I might have to ask Mom for a loan against next week's allowance. All Skylar comes up with is fifty-three cents.

The gas station is off-brand and pretty run down. No cars in the parking lot, no air-conditioning inside, a cooler full of water, soda, and beer. We pay the guy at the register one dollar and thirty cents, including tax, for two bottles of water. Luckily there's a two-for-one sale or we wouldn't have had enough.

If I had more money, I'd buy an extra and pour it over my head. That would feel so good.

Before we leave, Skylar asks the guy how far it is to the town limits.

He looks up from a hot rod magazine and says, "Huh?"

"The town limits," she says. "You know, where Evansburg ends and Newton starts."

"How should I know? I don't live around here." He goes back to his magazine, and we leave.

"Moron," says Skylar. "It can't be much farther. Remember the sign we saw for Newton—three miles?"

"Yeah, yeah, yeah." I sit beside her on a bus stop

bench that's been spray-painted with so much graffiti, I can't tell what color it is. A bank across the street has a big red thermometer on the side that reads 96 horrible degrees.

We sip our water and try to make it last. My bottle feels cold, so I press it against my forehead, hoping it will cool me off, but it doesn't.

Just as we're getting ready to leave, a beat-up red pickup slows down long enough for the driver to bang on his door and yell something gross at us.

Skylar scowls at the truck as it speeds away. "I hate guys like that." She finishes her water and gets on her bike. "Let's go before he comes back."

I look at her, suddenly worried. "Do you think he will?"

"Maybe. He's a perv, isn't he? Yelling things like that at twelve-year-olds."

My skin feels tight, itchy, like I'm getting heat rash or something. I don't like this part of town. I don't like this gas station with its old gas pumps and its garbage overflowing the dumpster. It stinks in the heat like somebody's cooking rotten food. Most of all, I don't like the guy in the pickup.

I take one last mouthful of water and swirl it around before I swallow it. "Let's go home," I say. "This place creeps me out."

Skylar squeezes a few more drops of water out of her bottle and tosses it into the trash can. "We're riding to the town limits," she says. "You agreed."

"Why? There won't be anything to see."

"How do you know? We've never seen the exact end of Evansburg." Skylar looks annoyed. Heat does that to her.

"Suppose our mothers find out?"

"How will they know?" Skylar asks. "Mom never cares where I am, as long as I'm home for dinner, and your mom's at work. We'll be back before she comes home."

"She'll find out. She always does. I can't get away with anything, and you know it."

"Oh, Abbi, that's because you always tell the truth." Skylar makes it sound like a character defect.

"She isn't as easy to fool as your mom."

"You just need to fib sometimes, that's all." Skylar straddles her bike and waits for me to get on mine. She pushes off, and I follow. I'm a little anxious, mostly about getting into trouble with Mom, but I follow Skylar to the top of another hill.

She zooms down the other side ahead of me, her hands high in the air. I let go of my handlebars. The bike picks up speed, and I feel the rush of air in my face. Not so long ago I was scared to ride no hands, but

Skylar has made me more reckless. Not as reckless as she is, but more reckless than my mom thinks I am.

We stop to rest beside a street sign for Marie Drive. A dead-end sign leans to the left beside it, like it's too tired to stand up straight.

"I've always wondered what's at the end of a dead-end street," Skylar says. "It's kind of like a riddle."

Even though my legs are tired and my T-shirt is soaked with sweat, I get back on my bike and follow her down Marie Drive. We cruise past a row of little ranch-style houses side by side, one after another, as tightly packed as a brand-new box of building blocks. Chain-link fences separate each green lawn from the one next to it.

It's as ordinary as our neighborhood, I think, and even more boring because it's so new and tidy and sort of unlived in. No one walks a dog. No kids play in the yards. No one mows grass or weeds the garden. All I hear is the hum of air conditioners. It's weirdly quiet, almost like it's under a spell.

I can't imagine Slap Your Face living in a little brick house with flowers in the front yard. Or Jason or Carter either.

After we leave the ranches behind, the houses get bigger and older. Weeds grow in some of the yards. We're in Slap Your Face territory for sure. I keep an eye out for her angry red face and squinty eyes, but all I see is a woman sitting on a porch. She watches us go by, as if she's been waiting for us to come along and put on a show for her.

Skylar says, "Maybe we should entertain her with some wheelies."

Dogs to beware of come out from under porches and hurl themselves against sagging chain-link fences. They snarl and bark and growl at us. We pump up speed and leave them behind, still barking. They look like the kind of dogs Carter and Jason might own—trained to kill.

At the bottom of a hill, we skid around a curve and Marie Drive turns into a rutted dirt road. A few houses, shabby and mysterious, hide way back in the trees. You can't tell if people live in them or not, but if someone does, you might not want to meet them. Rusty mailboxes lean this way and that. Some hang open like nobody's gotten any mail for a long time.

I expect Jason and Carter to jump out from the weeds and throw rocks at us. They'd have their dogs with them. Barking ferociously, the dogs would chase our bikes and bite our legs while Jason and Carter laughed.

If I were with anyone else, I'd turn around right now and go home. But I don't want Skylar to know

I'm scared of those houses, and the kids who might or might not live in them, so I keep my mouth shut and keep pedaling. I really don't care what's at the end of a dead end anymore. Or what's beyond the town limits. All I want is to see a road with a familiar name and follow it home.

A few minutes later Marie Drive stops at a wooden barrier painted with diagonal yellow and black stripes. On the other side is a field of waist-high weeds. A trail of ruts made by cars leads across the field to the woods on the other side. Even though people must use it sometimes, it's not a real road, so I declare it the official end of Marie Drive.

Skylar stares across the field, saying, "It's hardly worth riding all this way." We let our bikes fall on their sides, and we collapse in the shade of a huge oak tree.

"I sure wish I hadn't drunk all my water," I say.

"The next time we take a long bike ride," Skylar says, "we should bring a gallon jug."

I lean against the tree and look up into its branches. High over my head, I see what looks like a platform. I nudge Skylar. "Is that a tree house?"

"Where?" Skylar peers up, and I point. "Wow," she says. "Let's find a way to climb up there."

On the other side of the tree, a few old pieces of wood are nailed to the trunk like a ladder. Skylar reaches for one and hangs from it to test her weight. The nails hold. I inch my way up the tree behind her.

Once we're high enough to grab a branch, we abandon the ladder and climb from limb to limb like monkeys.

Skylar and I have had a lot of practice doing this. When we were nine or ten, we climbed every tree in our neighborhood. We even built a flimsy little tree house at the end of our street where we thought no one would notice. It was just big enough for us to sit in and read on hot summer days.

For a few weeks it had been our secret place. We even talked about finding a way to spend the night there. But before we could do it, our neighbor saw it and tore it down. Our mothers had no idea that the tree house Mr. Bowman called an eyesore was ours.

We never spoke to Mr. Bowman again. We even crossed the street if we saw him coming. At night we dared each other to knock on his door and run. Other times we ran around his house yelling. Once he actually chased us, but we could run lots faster than he could.

Last year, Mr. Bowman's daughter moved him to a nursing home. Skylar still hates him. I feel kind of sorry for him. He was mean to us, but now he's old and sick, so how can she hate him? "It's easy," Skylar said. "He tore down our tree house."

We hoist ourselves onto the platform. This tree

house is bigger and much better built than ours was. The wood is solid. We sit down and look way out across the field. From up here I see where the train tracks cross a stream and disappear into the woods. The sunlight is dazzling bright on the tracks and the water. In the other direction I see the houses on Marie Drive.

"Do you think the tree house belongs to anyone?" I ask.

"Let's claim it," Skylar says. "We can hang out here."

"Our secret hideout," I say.

"No one will know where we are," Skylar says. "Not even your mother with her superpower eyes."

I love this idea because somebody, usually my mother, has always known where I am—maybe not the exact place, but close enough. School, home, church, the mall, the swimming pool, the library. But here Skylar and I are in unknown territory—what old maps call terra incognita.

We sit together quietly, awed by the idea of total privacy. There's not a person in sight. A couple of deer amble across the field. Squirrels play hide-and-seek in the branches above our heads. A train rumbles through the woods, blowing its whistle for the crossing in town where the old station used to be.

"This is so much higher than our old tree house," Skylar says. "You can see forever from here. I love it."

"Me, too." I rest my cheek against the tree trunk. It feels rough and alive, warm from the afternoon sun.

"Uh-oh." Skylar points across the field. "Somebody's coming."

Two faraway figures come out of the woods. We watch them walk toward us. When they're closer, we both groan.

"Carter and Jason." Skylar mutters a curse word she probably learned from her brother, Rob. "They aren't in jail after all."

We both hate Carter and Jason. Everybody does. They're in the same grade as we are, but we've never had a class with them.

They get in fights and pick on pitiful sixth-graders. They steal kids' lunch money and act up in the cafeteria. They say gross things to girls, the kind of stuff you pretend not to hear because—well, just because.

Bullies, that's what they are, mean and nasty and ugly.

If this is their tree house, we won't have a secret place after all. And we'll have one more reason to hate Carter and Jason.

As they approach, we lie flat on our bellies and peer over the edge of the platform. They walk right under the tree without looking up. They don't see us or our bikes. They're too busy arguing with each other.

"You better not tell anybody about this," Carter says to Jason. He's the bully in charge, tall and skinny, with a long, narrow face and small, mean eyes set too close to his nose. He tells Jason what to do, and Jason does it. The hit man, Skylar and I call him.

Jason's short and squat, built close to the ground. His face is round, and his chin kind of blends into his neck. He's as dumb as an empty tin can rolling down the road. He scuffs along, hands stuffed in his pockets. His baseball cap is pulled low, hiding his face.

All of a sudden Carter shoves Jason and almost knocks him down. "Keep your big mouth shut. I mean it. You're always blabbing stuff. One of these days you'll get us in trouble."

"Okay, okay," Jason mutters. "I won't say nothing about him or what he does. We got a good deal. Why mess it up? I'm not stupid."

"Could've fooled me," Carter says, fishing a pack of cigarettes out of his jeans pocket and lighting one. He doesn't offer the pack to Jason.

Tough guy, I think.

They walk up Marie Drive without talking and disappear from sight.

"Whoa. That was close." Skylar rolls over on her back and stares up at the leaves. "I wonder what their big secret is."

"Probably something totally boring," I say.

"I bet Jason would tell me."

"Why would he tell you anything?"

She laughs. "Because he's in love with me. Haven't you noticed the way he looks at me?"

I laugh too. In fact, we laugh so hard we almost fall out of the tree. "Are you serious?" I ask her.

She snorts a last laugh and says, "Yeah, I am serious. Just before vacation, he started leaving notes taped to my locker. You wouldn't believe how bad his spelling is."

"You never told me!"

"I didn't tell anyone. I just wadded them up and threw them away. It's so gross. If other kids found out, I'd never live it down." Skylar narrows her eyes at me. "Promise you won't tell, Abbi."

"Of course I won't." I check the time on my phone. "Oh, no. It's after four already. I'll never beat Mom home."

We climb down and pull our bikes out of the weeds. Skylar starts pedaling toward Marie Drive, but I stop her. "That's the way Jason and Carter went. What if we catch up with them?"

"Good thought." She consults her phone. "There's a road just before the paved part of Marie Drive starts. It goes over the train tracks and ends at Brooke Street. We know how to get home from there."

"But what if that's the way *they* go?" I say.

We turn onto Barn Lane, another unpaved road. Unfortunately, the map on Skylar's phone doesn't mention the hills that stretch ahead of us. Or the fields with no trees and no shade, just cows watching us pedal past.

It's much longer than the way we came. We're hot and tired and irritable to the point where we argue about everything. Skylar says she wants a Coke, I say Pepsi's better. I say I love honeysuckle, Skylar says it's an invasive weed, and so on and on. By the time we get home, we're barely speaking to each other.

It's after five, and Mom's car is in the driveway. Skylar slings her bike down on her lawn beside Rob's dirt bike and goes inside her house without waving goodbye. Just as I'm getting ready to do the same with my bike, Mom pops out the front door.

"Stop right there and put your bike away properly," she says. "Do you want someone to steal it?"

I'm way too tired to argue. She sounds crosser than usual, like she's had a bad day at the bank. Or got caught in heavy traffic on the way home.

I pick up my bike and walk it to the garage. There are times when I wish Mom was more like Skylar's mom. Ms. Freeman is so casual about stuff. She doesn't care where the bikes are, as long as they're in the yard. It's the same inside. Clothes, books, and junk all over the place. Dust balls under the beds big enough to swallow a cat. Unwashed dishes in the sink. Nobody nagging you to pick this up and put that where it belongs. Ms. Freeman doesn't have proper places. Things belong where you leave them.

Skylar doesn't even make her bed. Why should she? She'd just have to make it again the next day. Unproductive use of time, she says.

It's a wonder Ms. Freeman and Mom are friends. Maybe opposites really do attract. Or maybe they bonded because they're both single moms. Who knows how adult minds work?

The second I come inside, Mom says, "Where have you been? I expect you to be here when I come home."

I ask myself, *What would Skylar do?* Without looking at Mom, I say, "I'm sorry. We were at the park watching some kids play baseball, and we forgot the time."

Mom sighs. "Just don't make a habit of it." She swats me on the butt to show me it's okay but I'd better not do it again. "Go wash up. Your face is all sweaty and your hands are dirty."

I head for the bathroom and lean against the door for a second. I fooled her. She believed me. I don't know whether to feel good or bad about it, but if I'd told the truth, there'd be no more bike rides to the tree house.

After dinner I text Skylar.

Hi, it's me. Are you still mad?

Nope. Are you?

No way.

Tree house tomorrow?

Sure.

We sign off with some funny emojis. I get in bed with my iPad and stream a science fiction series about the end of the world after a plague, which I hope will never happen, but maybe I should be prepared in case it does. If you expect the worst, it won't happen. At least that's what I like to think.

2

Skylar shows up around eleven. I've got two bottles of water in my backpack, along with peanut butter sandwiches and a couple of apples for Skylar and me in case she forgets to bring lunch. I also have *Never Let Me Go*, one of the books on our summer reading list.

My backpack is hot and heavy on my shoulder, but I'll have enough water for the ride home. Skylar never worries about stuff like dehydration, but I've read enough to know you can die of heat exhaustion in weather like this.

Her mom waves to us from the front porch. "Have fun, girls," she calls. "And be sure to come home before five, Abbi."

I glance at Skylar. "Your mom called last night," she says, "and told my mom to keep a better eye on you."

My face burns with embarrassment. It's not like Ms.

Freeman is my babysitter. She's a kindergarten teacher, so she has summers off. The bank is open all year round, so Mom doesn't. She has an arrangement with Ms. Freeman to keep an eye on me. Now it seems my mom is expecting Ms. Freeman to make sure I'm home before five. Considering how long she's been friends with Ms. Freeman, she should know that Skylar's mom isn't likely to notice what I do any more than she notices what Skylar or Rob do.

We leave our neighborhood and coast downhill to Grant Road. At the old railroad station, now a fancy restaurant, we turn down a narrow road, hardly more than a path, that runs along the train tracks. A sign says For Railroad Use Only, but we ignore it. We're pretty sure it's a shortcut to the tree house.

In the heat, the air smells like grease and cinders and tar. Old boxcars sprayed all over with graffiti sit on rusty tracks that go nowhere. Plastic bags and fast-food wrappers, empty cans and bottles litter the ground. Sometimes I think places like this are a preview of the future. All the people will be dead or gone, but their trash will be here forever.

Nobody's on the road but us. Skylar starts singing "I've Been Working on the Railroad," a song we learned in grade school. It seems like a good one for today. I join in, but I'm off-key as usual. Skylar doesn't care. She has a beautiful voice and carries the tune for both of us. We finish up with a loud chorus of "Fee fi fiddly i oh."

Skylar laughs. "Remember when we were in glee club and we had to sing for an assembly and Ms. Faglioni asked you not to sing, but just move your lips?"

I laugh, even though at the time Ms. Faglioni really hurt my feelings, and everyone, including Skylar, laughed at me. But still, it isn't like I wanted to be a pop singer or anything like that.

We ride along, feeling the heat now. There's not a single tree in railroad wasteland, and no shade. I want to drink my water but know I should save it for later. But what if I get hyperthermia? Maybe I should take a few sips, just in case.

Like she's reading my mind—which we both sometimes do with each other—Skylar stops and pulls out her water bottle. I watch her take a long drink, at least half of it. I remind myself that I have an extra bottle and follow her example. Water never tasted so good.

We've come to the bad part of the road. The tracks cross a bridge over the Paint Branch, a wide, mostly shallow stream of muddy water that never smells good. A narrow boardwalk runs along one side of the bridge, maybe put there for railroad workers. We get off our bikes and walk them across. The whole time, I worry that a train will come. Something might stick out of the train and hit us. Or the weight of the engine might bounce us off the boardwalk and we'll fall in the Paint Branch and catch a deadly disease from its polluted water.

I tell myself I'm just making up something new to worry about. If I made a list of my worries, it would stretch from here to California.

We cross without a train coming. The woods close in around us. Leaves block the sunlight, but somehow it's hotter and more humid in the shade. There's a horrible smell, like something died.

Skylar is ahead of me. Crows fly up into a tree and perch on its branches, cawing and flapping their wings in a menacing way.

Suddenly Skylar stops. "A dead deer's making that smell."

I pull up beside her. I don't want to, but I look at the deer, as if I must see what Skylar sees. It's lying on its side, its neck curved, its head back. What's left of the only eye I can see is looking right at us.

The crows have been tearing at it with their sharp beaks. Overhead, they mutter to each other and pace back and forth on the branches. A murder—that's what you call a flock of crows. A murder. It's a good name. You don't think of crows in flocks.

Skylar pedals ahead, fast. I follow her, pumping

hard. The smell clings to our clothes, to our hair. Hot spit floods my mouth and I almost throw up.

I hate the woods even more than the gas station. They're dark and damp and creepy. It's like a sort of darkness clings to the trees. Deer die here, crows eat them, but worse things than that happen. I don't know how I know. I just have a feeling.

"Where's the field?" I shout at Skylar. "We should have seen it by now." I look over my shoulder. A person can get lost so easily, especially in the woods, when everything is green and thick and you can't see very far. Skylar stops and looks around. The smell lingers. I can still hear the crows somewhere behind us.

"We couldn't have missed it," Skylar says. "It must be farther than we thought."

I ride slowly, looking for the field. I stop to read a faded sign nailed to a tree. I'm hoping it says something helpful, like *This Way to Marie Drive*, but no, of course not. It says Private Property. No Hunting or Fishing. It's riddled with bullet holes. What kind of person shoots signs?

Skylar has gotten ahead of me. She looks back and says, "Come on, Abbi! I see the field."

I follow her out of the woods and into the sunlight. Across the field is the end of Marie Drive and our tree house. We ride fast, bouncing over ruts and bumps.

Grasshoppers jump out of our way. I glance over my shoulder and tell myself there's nothing to be scared of. Deer die all the time. A murder of crows makes a lot of noise. People shoot holes in signs for the fun of it. I've got to stop being scared of stuff. Be more like Skylar and laugh things off.

It's a little cooler in the tree house. The leaves over our heads give us plenty of shade. A breeze dries our sweaty faces. We drink the rest of our open bottles of water and take out our books from the summer reading list. Some of them are long and hard, some short and easy. Skylar tends to pick the shorter ones. She's reading *The Hunger Games* now, which she's already read twice. It's not cheating, she says, because every time she reads it, she notices something she missed the other times.

I'm reading *Never Let Me Go*. So far it's pretty good. These kids live in an upscale orphanage or boarding school. I'm not sure which. When I checked it out, the librarian told me not to tell anyone about the big surprise. So far, I haven't come to that part, but when I do I'll keep it secret. I hate it when people give the plot away and ruin the whole book.

Suddenly Skylar nudges me. "Get down. A car's coming."

We stretch out on our stomachs and look down at

the road. A black SUV slows to a stop and parks right under our tree. A couple of minutes later, a little gray car pulls in behind it, the kind you see everywhere. No matter what make they are, they all look the same to me.

A woman gets out of the car. I can't see her face, because she's wearing huge sunglasses and a granny-style wide-brimmed straw hat. She gets into the SUV. Its tinted windows hide the driver, but I know it's a man when he says, "Hey, you—going my way?"

She laughs and shuts the passenger door. The SUV makes a U-turn and heads back up Marie Drive.

"What's that all about?" I ask Skylar.

She studies the gray car. "Maybe the woman is married and she's meeting the man in secret. Or maybe he's the one who's married. Or they both could be married—to other people."

"That's boring," I say. "It would be more interesting if they're criminals or spies."

"Like that TV show about the Russian spies who pretended to be ordinary Americans," she says. "I loved their disguises. It's amazing how different a wig can make you look."

"Russians really do spy. They even poison people," I say. "They hack into computers and all sorts of stuff."

Skylar stretches out on her back, hands behind her

head. "Remember back in the days of Nancy Drew, when we played detective?"

I laugh. "We really thought we'd catch a crook and become famous girl detectives. Like Nancy, of course."

"But the people we followed always turned out to be ordinary boring adults." Skylar rolls over and stares down at the gray car. "Those people are definitely not ordinary. They're up to something."

She leans toward me and lowers her voice, even though no one's in sight. "What if they really *are* spies? What if this is the mystery we were looking for when we were kids?"

"The woman definitely doesn't want anyone to recognize her," I say. "That ugly hat, those huge sunglasses."

Skylar frowns at the chipped polish on her thumbnail. "He could be a cheater like my dad."

She hasn't talked about her dad in ages. I thought she'd gotten over him, but I guess she's still mad. He walked out when she was eight or nine, so she has tons of bad memories.

Maybe it's better that I don't remember my dad. He left before I was born, and I've never even seen him, not a photograph, not a name. Unlike Skylar's mom, my mother never talks about him. Not even if I ask her. Sometimes I wonder if she got me from a sperm bank.

Anyway, I have no feelings for him one way or another. When I'm older, I plan to get a copy of my birth certificate.

I take a chance Skylar might get mad at me and say, "You don't know they're cheating. You don't know anything about them."

"Why else would they be meeting at a dead-end road where they think nobody will see them?"

"This isn't about your dad, Skylar, it's about solving a mystery. We decided they're Russian spies, remember? They're meeting here to exchange secrets or plan some kind of mission. They could even be terrorists, with explosives in the SUV."

She's picking a scab on her knee now, her face hidden by her hair. "So what do we do about it? How do we catch them with explosives or weapons or whatever? Especially when they have a car and we don't?"

"We'll video them," I say. "They'll never know they're being watched."

Skylar tosses her hair back and grins. "That's a great idea, Abbi! We'll get their license plate numbers, the make of their cars, the dates we see them. We might connect them to something we see on the news, a crime or a murder, and we'll have evidence."

We high-five each other. Skylar's totally on board with the spies, her dad forgotten.

"To the mystery we'll finally solve!" she says. We bump fists and drink some more water from my extra bottle.

"You take the videos, Abbi. Your phone has a better camera than mine. Take a few photos of her car now too, before they come back. Make sure you get the license plate."

I grab my phone and start gathering evidence for a crime that hasn't happened yet. I feel like a reporter covering a big story.

Skylar looks at my pictures. "These are great. The license plate is nice and sharp—Maryland 3MB5098."

"I'll take more when they come back," I say.

We open our lunch bags and eat our peanut butter sandwiches. While we're sharing mini Oreos from a bag, Jason and Carter slouch into sight. This time they come from Marie Drive and head across the field toward the woods. They have no idea we're watching them. I wonder if I've ever been watched without knowing it. A creepy thought.

"I wonder what they do in the woods." Skylar pulls her Oreo apart and licks the filling. "We should follow them. We might learn something interesting."

I look at her. "I don't care what they do in the woods. There's no way I'm following them anywhere."

Skylar goes on talking like I haven't said anything.

"Last night I got to wondering what they were arguing about yesterday—some sort of secret, a deal. I don't know, it just sounds interesting."

"Not to me. They're too stupid to do anything interesting."

"They must live around here," she says. "Probably in one of those old houses we passed."

We laugh. And I relax. Skylar's not saying we'll follow them today. We might not see them again. She might forget about it.

When we finish the Oreos, we eat our apples and read. It's really fun to be on my own, safe from bed making and dish washing and all the other boring chores on Mom's list. When I'm grown up, it will be like this most of the time. I'll be on my own every day.

Just as I'm getting kind of stiff from sitting so long, I see the SUV slow to a stop behind the gray car.

Skylar whispers, "They're back."

I look down. If only the SUV had a sunroof, we could see the people inside. Or at least the tops of their heads.

The man and woman are talking but too softly for us to understand them. They could be saying I love you or they could be plotting to blow up a building or assassinate an enemy.

Skylar nudges me. "When she gets out of the car, take a video. We can watch it later in slo-mo and get a better look at her."

While the mysterious couple talk, I video the SUV, but leaves block my view of the license plate.

At last the door opens and I glimpse the back of a man's head as the woman gets out. Still wearing her hat and sunglasses, she says, "Love you. See you next Thursday."

"Love you, too," he says.

I video her getting into her car, making a U-turn, and driving away, her face still hidden.

The SUV waits a while, but after maybe five minutes it leaves. I get a shot of its license plate—Maryland 9PS4227—and a faded bumper sticker for the local radio station.

When the SUV is gone, I say, "They love each other."

"Yeah," Skylar says.

"They're *spies*," I say, "not cheaters. Probably neither one of them is married."

Skylar frowns, but she doesn't argue.

We look at my video. It's kind of blurry because of the tree. "Does she look familiar to you?" I ask.

She shakes her head. "If only she'd take off those sunglasses and that stupid hat. We don't know what color her hair is or whether it's short or long."

"There's something about her," I say, toying with a memory. "The way she walks, maybe. But then probably lots of people look like her."

"Average height," Skylar says, "medium build. Not much to go on. But that's what makes her a good spy. Forgettable, you know?"

I swallow a mouthful of water. "Let's make sure to be here next Thursday."

We bump fists, pack up our stuff, and climb down the tree.

"Train tracks or Marie Drive?" Skylar asks.

I hesitate. "The train tracks are faster, but the woods are creepy. We'd have to pass the deer."

"No hills, though," Skylar says. "No cars."

She turns toward the field, and we ride through the leaping grasshoppers again. A cloud drifts across the sun and the woods turn dark. We slow down. I'm not sure we made the right choice. But then the cloud floats away and the woods are just trees in the sunlight.

Soon after we pedal into the woods, a deer steps in front of us. She's small, not quite full grown. She still has white spots on her fur. For a moment she freezes and stares at us, wide-eyed. We brake to a stop and sit quietly. The deer looks at us. We look at the deer. It's magic.

Suddenly her ears turn and twitch as if she hears something we can't. She bounds away. The white flag of her tail vanishes into the underbrush.

I hear a noise behind us. Skylar and I whirl around. Jason and Carter are standing a few feet away. Carter points his finger like a gun at the place the deer disappeared. "Pow!"

He and Jason laugh, but Skylar and I tighten our grip on our handlebars. I feel like the deer, frozen.

"What are you doing here?" Carter asks us. His voice has a nasty edge that slides under my skin like a knife.

Jason sniggers and stares at Skylar. Carter lights a cigarette and says, "You girls smoke?"

We shake our heads. They haven't threatened us yet, but it's like waiting for lightning when the air feels electric.

"They don't smoke," Carter tells Jason in a prissy little voice. "They're too good for us."

"They're in *Honors*," Jason says.

Carter sneers. "They're *dogs*."

All around us, the woods are still. The air is hot and humid, so thick it's hard to breathe. There's no one here but us and them.

Jason takes hold of Skylar's handlebars. "You want to have some fun with me and Carter? There's this old house on Marie Drive. Kids party there at night, but nobody's there now."

Carter rests his hand on my arm. I jerk away from him.

Jason tightens his grip on Skylar's handlebars, and Carter blocks me. I'm sweating so much I feel it run down my sides.

"These girls are dogs," Carter says again. "Maybe we should take their bikes and let them walk home."

Carter makes a move to grab my backpack, and I duck away. My feet tangle in the pedals and the bike and I topple over.

I scramble to my feet. Blood is running down my leg from a cut.

Carter blows cigarette smoke in my face. "Bowwow, ugly doggy."

I jump back on my bike, and we break away from them, pumping the pedals as hard as we can.

"Go home, dogs," Carter yells. "And don't come back."

We pick up speed, but I can still hear them yelling disgusting things at us. We pass the dead deer again. It smells even worse than before. The crows caw, their eyes glitter, their beaks are sharp and bloody. I almost throw up again, but I keep going, splashing through puddles, skidding on cinders, scared the boys will come after us.

When we're out of the woods, we slow down to cross the bridge. We're both breathing hard. Blood runs down my leg and stains my shoe, but we don't stop again until we're in sight of Main Street.

"Dogs." Skylar clenches her teeth. "They called us *dogs.* I hate them."

We dump our bikes on the sidewalk. There's a drinking fountain outside the old train station. We wipe our noses and drink some water. Then we sit on a bench and rest. We're both too shaky to get back on our bikes right away.

"Hey." Skylar's brother coasts toward us on his racing bike. He brakes and stares at us. "What happened to your leg, Abs? You're bleeding all over the place. Are you okay?"

"She fell off her bike," Skylar says quickly.

"Skidded on some gravel," I tell him, suddenly shy. He's been having an odd effect on me lately, maybe because he's gotten taller all of a sudden and much cuter.

"Looks nasty," Rob says. "Better go home and get it cleaned up. Otherwise it might get infected and they'll amputate your leg." He laughs to show he's joking. But what happened isn't funny.

"That's where I'm going." I'm embarrassed to look at him. I can feel myself blushing and I don't even know why.

"I'm going with her," Skylar says.

As soon as Rob's out of sight, I say, "You told me Jason loves you." It sounds like an accusation. "He sure doesn't act like it."

Skylar snorts in disgust. "He has to look tough for Carter. He's so pathetic."

We get back on our bikes and ride fast, pumping hard to get home as quick as possible. I have half an hour to clean myself up before Mom comes home. I wash my cut and cover it with a Band-Aid. I scrub the blood off my shoe and sock, comb my hair, and wash my face. By the time Mom arrives, I'm sitting on the couch reading *Never Let Me Go*. You'd think I'd been there all day.

3

Skylar and I decide to skip the tree house for a few days. We don't want to run into Carter and Jason anytime soon. Maybe we'll go only on Thursdays, when the mystery couple meets.

The next day, Skylar and I make ourselves comfortable in lawn chairs in her backyard and read. It's a hot, lazy day, the cicadas are buzzing somewhere in the trees overhead, and someone is cutting the grass with an old-fashioned push mower.

A few yards away, Rob's working on his bike in the driveway. I can't help taking secret looks at him. I wish I could ask Skylar if he has a girlfriend, but if she suspected I like him, she'd pretend she was going to tell him, maybe even actually do it, and tease me endlessly about how her brother is a secret slob who talks with his mouth full and watches cartoons on TV even though he's seventeen—proof that he's a moron.

In all honesty, it's pretty ridiculous. Rob will be a senior in the fall. He's on the football team and the basketball team. Plus he's tall and blond and good-looking in the same way Skylar is. A crush on him is like falling in love with a rock star. Impossible, hopeless, stupid.

After a while Rob stops working on his bike, goes inside, and comes out with three cans of soda. He hands one to Skylar and one to me.

I thank him, but Skylar stares at hers like it might explode. "What's the catch?" she asks.

"There's no catch. I'm just being polite, that's all." He reaches for the can. "If you don't want it, I'll drink it."

Skylar opens the can. "That's okay, I'll keep it."

I watch her drink. What's going on with her and Rob? It's like she's always mad at him. If I had a big brother as nice as he is, I wouldn't treat him that way. Rob sits on the grass facing us. "If you guys keep on reading all the time, I swear you'll turn into books."

"You should try it," Skylar says. "You might learn something."

He gives her the sort of look Skylar gives me when I'm being really irritating. *Twins born five years apart*, I think.

"What's going on, Sky?" he asks. "You get up on the wrong side of the bed or something?"

Skylar makes an exasperated noise. "Come on, Abbi, let's go to your house. We can read in peace there. Even turn into books if we want to."

Rob finishes his soda and lies down on the grass, his eyes shut. "Sisters," he mutters.

After Skylar and I cross the street, I say, "Why are you mad at Rob?"

"You don't want to know," she says. "He's not as great as you think he is, I can tell you that."

"You were really rude to him. Did you have a fight or what?"

We go into my house and shut the door. Skylar looks at me, and I see she's not mad after all. She's worried.

"What if I told you I found a bag of pot in his bureau drawer?"

"It must be something else. Rob would never do anything that stupid." My mouth hangs open like I'm stunned.

"It was pot, Abbi. Everybody in middle school knows what it smells like." She swipes her hair behind her ears. "Rob is a stoner."

"I don't believe you," I say. "Stoners don't play football."

"You are so naive," Skylar says.

"I am not!" This isn't the first time she's told me

that. It's getting on my nerves. What does she know that I don't know?

We stare at each other. The clock on the mantel ticks. Shadows of leaves dance across the walls, changing shape in the breeze. Then Skylar flops down on the sofa, opens *The Hunger Games*.

I sit next to her, *Never Let Me Go* unopened in my lap. "Did you tell him you found the pot?" I'm hoping she'll say no, and then I can pretend it belongs to someone else and Rob is just keeping it safe for them.

She shakes her head. "It's not like I saw him steal a candy bar at Madison Market. This is big. He could get kicked off the team and ruin his whole life." Skylar looks like she might cry. "He knows I'm mad at him, but he doesn't know why."

"What if the pot belongs to someone else and he's just keeping it for them or something?"

She sniffs and wipes her nose with the back of her hand. "He sneaks out at night," she says, "after Mom goes to bed."

"Where does he go?"

"I don't know!" Now Skylar is getting mad—at me? At Rob? Whatever—it's time to stop asking questions.

"I'm hungry," I say. "There's tuna salad in the fridge. We can make sandwiches."

By the time we've finished the sandwiches and

topped them off with a pint of mint chocolate chip ice cream, Skylar is back to normal. We sit down and read again. Even though I want to know more about Rob, I keep my mouth shut. She's put him in the place where she keeps things she doesn't want to talk about.

A few days later, Ms. Freeman drives us to the pool. To save time changing, we wear shorts over our bathing suits. We both hate the dressing room. The cement floor is always wet and the cubicles have these cheap curtains that never stay together. People are always opening them to see if anyone is in there. Somehow they pick the exact moment you're naked or half naked and say, "Oops, sorry, I thought this one was empty."

After Skylar and I pay, we go straight to the pool, fold our shorts, and lay them on our towels. We do what we always do first—dive into the deep end and race each other underwater to the other side. We come up at the same time, take a deep breath, and dive again. We race each other three times before Skylar wins by a hand.

We sit on the edge of the pool and look around to see who's here. Skylar really likes this boy named Jonathon, but we don't see him. "He might go to the country club pool. He lives on the best side of town," she says.

"Where do we live?"

"Somewhere in the middle. Not rich, not poor."

I notice some girls in our class at the kiddy pool. I nudge Skylar. "Look. Mr. Boyce is here with his wife and baby."

Skylar jumps up. "Where?"

"Over there with Lindsey and Nessa and Erica. Let's say hi."

Almost every seventh-grade girl loves Mr. Boyce. He's tall and super good-looking, and he teaches language arts, Skylar's and my favorite subject this year.

We tug our bathing suits into place top and bottom, smooth our hair, and casually join the group.

"Well, well." Mr. Boyce grins at us, and his white teeth flash. "It's Skylar and Abbi, the one and only super-duper dynamic duo."

My heart zooms a little. I like Mr. Boyce soooo much, I don't know what to say. So I just sit on the edge of the wading pool, gazing at him.

"Have you two met my wife, Rose?" he asks, like we're grown-ups entitled to know his wife's first name.

We shake our heads, and he introduces us. Even though she must be at least thirty, Rose is still pretty.

Mr. Boyce hoists the baby over his head and the baby chuckles. "This is my son, Andrew Junior—Andy for short."

Skylar and I ooh and aah over the baby, maybe because he looks so much like Mr. Boyce. We love him, he's adorable. Maybe we can babysit for him someday.

Lindsey leans forward and raises her hand like she's in school. "Mr. Boyce, Mr. Boyce," she calls. "Why aren't you teaching eighth-grade English next year? All the other teachers are mean and strict and grumpy."

"Yes," Nessa adds. "We need you, Mr. Boyce."

The rest of us gather around him. "Please teach eighth grade," we beg. "Please, please, please."

He laughs. "There's nothing wrong with the eighth-grade English teachers," he says.

"They aren't *you*," Skylar says.

"Oh, you girls are so sweet. I should have flunked every one of you and made you take my class all over again."

He laughs, but Mrs. Boyce picks up Andy and frowns at her husband. "It's past time for Andy's nap," she says. "We have to go. Get the blanket and towels."

"Sorry, girls." Mr. Boyce begins to fold the blanket. I pick up Andy's little yellow duck and a couple of plastic boats and hand them to my teacher.

"Thanks, Abbi."

We watch him follow his wife to the car. You can tell that Mrs. Boyce is mad by the way she slaps one foot down after the other, like she's squashing bugs.

"Wow," Nessa says, "what a crab."

Lindsey shakes her head. "Poor Mr. Boyce."

"I bet they get divorced," Erica says.

Skylar sits beside me, examining her chipped

thumbnail polish again. I wonder if she's thinking about her dad.

The five of us go back to the pool and sit on the bottom to see who can hold their breath longest. I win three times in a row. Then we try to talk to each other underwater. That makes us laugh and snort and cough. We spread our towels on the grass and watch some boys we know cannonball off the diving board until the lifeguard blows his whistle and makes them stop.

Nessa and Lindsey think the boys are cute, but Erica, Skylar, and I think they're jerks. Not as bad as Carter and Jason, of course, but the kind that think making farting noises is really funny.

By the time Ms. Freeman shows up, our noses are bright red and our arms and legs are pink and we're ready for a quick stop at Shake Shop for Mango Passionades.

We go to the pool almost every day, but we don't see Mr. Boyce again. We decide that his wife didn't like the way we hung around him. "Maybe she's jealous," Nessa says, but that's totally ridiculous. Why would a grown woman be jealous of twelve-year-old girls? She must just want him all to herself. He sees enough of us at school. Now it's summer, and it's her turn.

4

On Thursday, Skylar and I ride our bikes back to Marie Drive. The gray car shows up right on schedule, and this time the SUV parks behind it. The woman gets into the SUV and they drive away together just like last week. I video everything, but we still can't see their faces. The man doesn't get out of his SUV, and the woman doesn't take off her sunglasses or her hat.

"Let's look in her car," Skylar says. "Maybe we'll see something that gives us a clue."

I'm not sure this is a good idea. "What if they come back while we're looking?"

"They just left, Abbi. They won't be back for a couple of hours." Skylar begins climbing down the tree.

I follow her. I know she's probably right, but I keep thinking of scary movies where the bad guy leaves but then forgets something and comes right back.

Skylar goes straight to the car and peers into the passenger window, but I sort of creep up like it's going to explode if I touch it.

On the back seat, there's a yoga bag and a large book with the title *A Guide to Abstract Expressionism.* An empty water bottle sits in the driver's cup holder. On the passenger seat is a pink hoodie from the Gap. Her car is so old it actually has a CD player. A few discs by jazz musicians are scattered on the seat.

I take pictures of everything. You can never tell what's important.

We climb back up to the tree house and eat our lunch. "So have we learned any new stuff about the mystery woman?" Skylar asks.

"She takes yoga, she likes art and jazz," I say, "and she buys clothes at the Gap. Like a good spy, she doesn't give away anything personal."

"Did you notice that one of the CDs was by a musician with a Russian name?"

I look at the picture I took of the CDs—one is called *Meditation on a Theme.* "Definitely Russian," I say.

Skylar opens a bag of mini Oreos and takes a handful. "Here. Have some."

A squirrel watches us eat. His bright eyes focus on the cookies. I toss him the half without icing. He holds it in his little paws and nibbles daintily. A couple of his pals scurry from branch to branch and climb headfirst down the tree trunk toward us. We toss crumbs to keep them happy.

A huge flock of black birds swirls past, not crows but starlings, changing direction, veering right, veering left, soaring up, sweeping down as if one brain controls all of them. A murmuration, my mother calls it. She claims it's good luck to see one.

I stretch out my legs. My kneecaps pop up like hills. Skylar's lucky to have straight legs with muscles instead of bumpy knees and bony shins. I watch her read and wish I looked just like her. Today we're wearing matching outfits we bought at Target, something we do sometimes. My T-shirt has narrow blue stripes to match my shorts. Skylar has red stripes to match her shorts. Even though our clothes are the same, hers look much better on her than mine do on me. I remind myself that I'll be thirteen three months before her. And that I'm better in drawing and language arts than she is, but only slightly—the difference between an A minus and a B plus.

She glances up, like she knows I'm looking at her, and grins. I grin back but immediately feel terrible. What kind of person is jealous of her best friend?

We read for a while longer, but we're distracted by voices. We're surprised to see Rob and three of his friends riding their bikes across the field toward Marie Drive. They're talking and laughing and paying no attention to their surroundings. As soon as they're gone, Skylar scrambles to her feet and starts climbing down. "Come on, let's follow them."

I can't explain it, but I don't think this is a good idea. Of course there's no use telling Skylar that. Not when she's already waiting for me on the ground.

Even though Rob and his friends are out of sight by now, we leave our bikes behind and walk along the edge of Marie Drive, keeping to the bushes in case they suddenly appear. We stop at a driveway, almost hidden in weeds.

Skylar points to bike tracks in the dirt. "They went up here."

Darting from tree to tree, we sneak up the drive. It's like playing detective again, just the way we used to.

Finally we see the house. Or what's left of it. Most of the roof has caved in. The rest is held up by vines growing on the walls.

A gust of air stirs the leaves and twitches the weeds. Somewhere, far away, thunder rumbles, but the sun is shining where we are.

They've hidden their bikes in an overgrown straggle of bushes and vines, but sunlight bounces off the handlebars. We crouch behind a tree and watch the house. We listen for voices. Except for a bird chirping in a bush by the door, the house is silent. No one walks past a window or door. We know the boys are in there. Where else could they be?

We make a fast dash across the yard and hide in a tangle of weeds and brambles, ready to run if we have to. A splintered piece of plywood lies on the ground. A Condemned sign is nailed to it.

Moments later, Jason and Carter ride up on shiny new dirt bikes, not the cheap ones you'd buy at Walmart, but the kind you see in a really expensive bike store like High Gear on Main Street. They must have stolen them.

"What are they doing here?" I whisper.

Skylar presses her finger to her mouth and shakes her head.

They lay their bikes down carefully and go inside. I notice that Jason has a backpack, not something he usually wears.

We expect Rob and his friends to ask them who they are and what they want, maybe even chase them away, but instead it sounds like they planned to meet the boys.

"Did you bring it with you?" Rob asks.

Skylar grabs my arm so tightly I wince. "I told you," she whispers.

No, no, no, I say in my head. *No, no, no.*

"Sure we did," Carter says.

"It's right here in my pack." That's Jason's voice.

"Good stuff at a good price."

"The best you can get," Carter adds.

"Where did you get it?" one of Rob's friends asks. "You look pretty young to be dealing anything stronger than chewing gum."

Rob and the others laugh, but Jason's face flushes. "You think we're stupid enough to tell you?" he asks.

"You buying or not?" Carter asks. "We can always sell it to somebody else. We got plenty of contacts."

"What do you guys think?" Rob asks his friends.

"Yeah, sure, let's do it."

"It's a deal then," Rob says.

"Okay," Jason says. I imagine him pulling out a bag, or whatever pot comes in, and handing it over.

"It looks good," Rob says. "Here, take a look, Woody. What do you think?"

"Awesome," the guy named Woody says. "You kids did all right."

"We might use you again," one of the others says.

"Where's the money?" Jason asks.

"Here you go," Rob says. "Just what you asked for. We'll call you when we need more."

Jason and Carter come outside and high-five each other. "Man, what suckers," Carter sneers. They jump on their fancy new bikes. Heads down, riding fast, they disappear around a curve in the driveway.

"Now do you believe me?" Skylar asks.

I nod, too depressed to say anything. Maybe Skylar's right. I was naive a few days ago, but not anymore. Now I know what she knows.

It's about then that the sky turns dark and rain starts falling fast and hard. Lightning flashes back and forth, pitchforking from one cloud to the next and then plunging straight down to earth. The thunder is like someone hitting you on the head. *Boom boom boom.*

We stay where we are, pressed against the side of the house, safe from lightning, I think. I hope. Rain pours off the roof like a waterfall. The trees are a green blur whipping back and forth in the wind, filling the air with leaves and twigs.

Inside the house is quiet. Pot smoke drifts out the window. Somebody laughs. I sink into silence so deep I can hardly breathe. Skylar has nothing to say either. The rain is cold. It soaks through our clothes. We shiver and hug ourselves to keep warm. I want to go home, but not in a lightning storm.

After a while, the rain lets up a little and Skylar grabs my hand. "Come on, let's make a run for it."

We sprint toward the driveway, but before we're halfway there, I hear Rob yell, "Skylar, what the hell are you doing here?"

She doesn't answer, doesn't stop, doesn't even look back, just keeps running, dragging me with her.

Rob catches up with us and grabs her arm, spinning

her around to face him. She lets go of me and I stagger to keep my balance. "Don't touch me, you druggie," she screams at Rob. "I hate you!"

"Calm down, Skylar, it's just pot. It's legal in some places now."

Rain pours down on us, thunder booms, lightning flashes in webs across the sky. I don't know which scares me more—the storm or Rob and Skylar fighting in the downpour, slipping in mud, yelling at each other.

Rob grabs Skylar's arm again and mine too. "Shut up and get in the house."

Skylar gives up and lets him drag us both inside. The place is moldy and nasty and full of trash. Rain splashes down through holes in the roof. It smells almost as bad as the dead deer.

I'd rather go outside and be struck by lightning than stay in this house, but Rob isn't about to let us leave.

"Listen to me, Skylar," Rob says. "Don't tell Mom. This is the first time I've ever bought drugs. Honest. It's for a big party."

"That's a lie," Skylar yells. "You've got a sock stuffed with pot in your bureau. I *saw* it!"

He shakes his head. "That belongs to somebody else. I was keeping it for him, not smoking it."

Even I don't believe that, not anymore.

"You liar," Skylar says. "I hate you, Rob. You're a dumb idiot."

A few guys I've seen with Rob are leaning against a wall, watching us. Like him, they play on the football team.

"Don't tell *anybody*," one says to Skylar and me. "It's no big deal, not like something you'd see in *Breaking Bad*. No killings, no drug lords, just small-town stuff."

Skylar stares him down. "If it's no big deal, why are you so scared we'll tell?"

Even though I know Rob and his friends won't hurt us, we're trapped in this house full of bad smells and secrets and horrible stuff written and drawn on the walls. It's worse than the scariest Halloween house I've ever seen, and I want to get out, go home, get in bed, and pretend none of this ever happened. Most of all, I never want to see Rob again. I hate him.

"It's like this, Sky," Rob says. "If you tell, the coach might find out and kick us off the team. This is senior year. Don't ruin it by blabbing to Mom like a little tattletale kid."

He glances at me shivering in my wet clothes and hating him so much. "That goes for you too, Abbi."

Skylar folds her arms across her chest. Her lips are blue with cold. "You're the one who's ruining it, not us."

"Just promise not to tell, I beg you, Skylar. That's all I'm asking." Rob's voice breaks, and I see how scared he is.

Skylar sees it, too. He's bossed her around all her life, teasing her, making her feel little and powerless. Now it's her turn to make him feel powerless.

She looks at me. I don't know what she wants me to say, so I just look at the floor and try not to cry.

"Please, Sky," Rob says. "Be a buddy. I'll pay you back somehow, I promise."

"Okay, okay," Skylar says. "Just shut up. I won't tell, but if you end up in jail, I won't visit you. And I won't care. I'll tell people I'm not related to you—and you know what? I'll wish it was true."

She turns to me. "Let's get out of here."

"Sky—" Rob calls after us. "Really, it won't happen again, I mean it. Don't be mad!"

She doesn't answer. I follow her outside. The rain has changed to a cold drizzle. Thunder rumbles in the distance and lightning dances overhead like small brushstrokes on the dark sky. We stop to get our backpacks from the tree house and pull our bikes out of the wet weeds.

The gray car is gone, its tire tracks filled with rainwater.

The ride home is long and silent. For once, Skylar

has nothing to say. She gets like that when she's really upset and doesn't want to talk about it. I know better than to say something.

What would I say, anyway?

5

Skylar and I stop for a minute in front of our houses. The street is littered with small branches and leaves blown down by the storm. There's a huge puddle in Skylar's driveway. The flowers in our yard are beaten down. They droop every which way, their blossoms hanging.

"Don't say anything to your mother about Rob," Skylar says.

I'm hurt to hear her say this. "Of course I won't tell her."

"She's wormed stuff out of you before."

"She won't this time, I swear."

Skylar stares into my eyes like she's looking for proof that I won't tell.

"Cross my heart, Skylar."

"See you tomorrow." She rides right through the

puddle, slings the bike on its side in the grass, and goes inside without looking at me.

I know it's Rob she's mad at, not me. But I feel bad anyway. At home, I strip off my clothes and take a shower. I stand in the stream of hot water and cry. I'm confused and upset. I don't know what to do or think or anything.

Secrets gnaw at me—the tree house, the man and woman in their cars, Jason and Carter, the horrible house, Rob and the drugs. Even the dead deer. I can't get its smell out of my nose or the way it looked at me out of my mind—its eye clouded over but staring right at me, its head bent back so its bloody throat showed. The flies that didn't even fly away, the crows hunched on branches, cawing at us.

How did Skylar and I get into so much scary trouble? We just wanted our own private place, that's all. And now it's like I'm trapped in a bad dream that I can't share with Mom. I have to pretend everything is fine. If she ever finds out what Skylar and I are up to, she'll kill me.

I sit on the couch and wait for her. She walks in, all smiles, and flops down beside me. "How about dinner tonight with Greg at Gepetto's Pizza?"

I force myself to smile and look happy, but as much as I love Greg, I'm not in the mood for him or pizza. I just want to go to bed and stream Disney videos until I fall asleep. But if I tell Mom that, she'll think I'm sick or that I quarreled with Skylar and she'll start asking questions. I might cry and break down and tell her everything.

So maybe it's good to be going out after all. Greg will be his usual funny self and make me laugh, and maybe I'll forget everything for a little while.

"He'll be here any minute," Mom says. "Can you be ready that fast?"

I tell her I'm ready now.

A couple of minutes later the doorbell rings. Greg gives us both a big hug. His beard rubs against my cheek and he smells good, like he just took a shower.

We ride in his work truck that has a big sign on the side advertising his plumbing business. Mom's up front with him, and I'm in the little seat behind them. Sometimes Skylar comes with us, and the two of us squeeze in together. Our elbows and knees bump. It's a tighter fit every year. Is the truck shrinking, Greg asks, or are Skylar and I growing? If we can't stay the same size, he says, he'll need to buy a bigger truck.

By the time we're sitting in a booth at Gepetto's, Greg has noticed how quiet I am.

He leans across the table. He has one arm around Mom, but his attention's on me. "Want to hear what happened to me today?"

I force a smile and nod. Greg tells great stories about the people he meets and the houses he sees. Before I met him, I had no idea a plumber's life was so exciting.

"Well, today I go see this lady whose sink is stopped up. The minute I walk in the door, I see cats everywhere, dozens of them, scrawny and ugly and hopping with fleas the size of mice. The furniture is all clawed up, but that's not the worst of it. The whole place stinks like the cats pee everywhere. I mean it's like I can hardly breathe. I'm coughing and choking. I need a gas mask or something."

He drinks some water and goes on. "She gives me this worried look and says, 'I hope you're not allergic to cats.' I want to say it's just their pee I'm allergic to, but I'm a nice guy, you know, I have my reputation to think of, so I just fix that sink as fast as I can. By the time I leave, I have tears in my eyes from the stink. I swear I still smell cat pee."

He sniffs his arm and holds it across the table toward me. "Can you smell it?"

I make a face. "Pee-yew. You really stink, Greg!" Everybody laughs, even me. I wonder, if I stick my arm out, will he smell the dead deer?

I'm beginning to feel better. Except for Rob and the pot, maybe things aren't so terrible after all. The man and woman aren't really spies, just two people who love each other. We don't know if they're married or not. They could have all sorts of reasons for meeting at Marie Drive.

The server comes over, and Greg orders a large pizza. "We'd like extra cheese, sausage, green peppers, and anything else the chef wants to throw on it."

"Mushrooms," Mom adds.

"No anchovies, please," I say.

The server looks like he goes to college. If Skylar was here, she'd flirt with him. She claims that she never flirts, she doesn't even know how. Maybe she really doesn't know she does it. Maybe it just comes naturally to her. But if she said *No anchovies, please*, the server would smile at her and say he hates anchovies, too. But when I say it, he just writes it down with the other stuff.

"So, Abbi," Greg says. "I told you what I did today. What did you do?"

"Nothing much. Skylar and I rode bikes, got caught in the rain, just boring summer vacation stuff." While I talk, I study the place mat, a map of Italy with a lot of Italian words written on it.

"Where did you go on your bikes?" Mom looks anxious. To her, the world is dangerous. She worries about lonely places and strangers and all the bad things that can happen. Her worries got passed to me in my DNA, kind of like a gift the wicked fairy might give you when you're christened.

"No place special," I tell her. "Just around town." I point to an Italian phrase on the place mat and ask Greg what it means. His mother was born in Italy, and he knows some Italian.

"*Essere l'altra metà della mela*,'" he reads.

The words are beautiful the way he says them. They sound like music. Maybe I'll take Italian in high school, but then I remember that French and Spanish are the only language choices.

"What does it mean?" I ask.

"The other half of the apple," he says. "You know, soul mates, like you and Skylar are two halves of the same apple."

Yes, Skylar and I are like that most of the time, though not always, especially lately.

Mom looks like she's about to ask for more details about the bike ride, but the server saves me by bringing our pizza.

Greg and Mom have a beer, and I have a soda. While we eat, Greg tells us another story about his life in plumbing land.

"The house looks okay from the outside," he says, "but inside, I can hardly get to the kitchen because of all the boxes and piles of books and newspapers and bulging black garbage bags in every room. I mean they're floor to ceiling, with little tunnels to get from one room to the next. Hoarders, I guess. I see a lot of that."

"How can people live that way?" Mom asks. "It's so dangerous."

Greg takes a swallow of beer. "I tell you, Cathy, you can drive down a nice street and never dream of what some of the houses look like inside. I've seen it all—places where the windows are clean and there's no dust on anything, and others where you need a gas mask or a shovel."

I think of Skylar's house and the mess in every room. Even when we were little, we always played at my house. I think she was embarrassed then and still is. It's no big deal to me.

After we leave Gepetto's, we stop at a Dairy Queen out on Route 203. It's the old-fashioned kind, with a walk-up window and no inside seating. Greg and Mom get sodas but my appetite is back and I order a peanut butter shake.

We carry our stuff to a picnic table. It's almost sunset. The shadows are long, and cicadas are tuning up for the night. The first star hangs in the sky, and I make a wish that Mom and Greg will get married. He's the only thing close to a father I've ever known, and I'm always afraid he might drift away.

While I slurp my shake, I notice Jason and Carter

in line at the walk-up window. I slump down and lower my head. *Please don't let them see me, please, please, please.*

Keeping my head down, I watch them. They're laughing and pushing each other in that dumb boy way. They bump the man in front of them. He turns and says, "Don't do that again, Jason." His voice has a really ugly edge, like he's angry.

"What's wrong with you?" Jason asks. "Geez, I was just kidding around."

The man is about Greg's age. He has muscles like he works out in a gym. His arms are inked in sleeves from his wrists to his shoulders. It's clear to me that no one should mess with him. But not to Jason.

The girl with him says, "Let it go, Paul." She's got tattoos too, but not as many as he does. Or maybe I just can't see them all. Her hair is dyed purple and blue, and she's got a stud in her nose.

"Maybe I don't like kidding." Paul shoves Jason so hard he staggers back and lands on the ground.

"Hey, that hurt!" Jason scrambles to his feet.

"Come on," Carter says to him. "Get your bike, let's go."

But Jason isn't ready to leave. He pulls away from Carter and steps close enough to Paul to stand toe to toe. He clenches his fists, and his face turns an ugly shade of red. "Don't push me like that again," he says.

Paul grabs Jason by the shirt. The snake tattoos writhe up and down his arms. "Keep it up and I'll punch your face in."

The girl tugs Paul's arm. "Can't we just have a nice night out?"

He shrugs her off. Carter has already backed away, but Jason scowls at the man.

Jason's in big trouble. Even though I don't like him, I'm scared of what Paul might do to him.

Just as I think Paul is going to hit Jason hard, Greg steps between them. "Hey, Paul, what's up?"

Paul looks at Greg. "What are you doing here, man?"

Carter yanks Jason away. Unfortunately, I've raised my head to watch what's going on, and they see me.

"What are *you* looking at?" Jason asks.

I think of some things I could say, but not with Mom sitting beside me. "Not much," I tell him. It's amazing how fast I've lost all sympathy for him.

Jason spits in the dirt, and he and Carter ride away on their bikes. It's getting dark, but do they have lights? Of course not.

"Do you know that boy?" Mom asks me.

"He goes to my school. Skylar and I hate him."

Before she can ask any more questions, Greg sits down with us. "Paul's got a nasty temper. He'd have punched that kid out."

Mom stares at Greg. "How do you know a guy like him?"

"I used to hire him as a backup if one of the guys on my crew was out sick or something. But he has issues. Drugs and stuff. I can't count on him to show up for work."

We finish our food and get into the truck. I look out the window. It's almost dark now, and the first star shines brightly. Venus, the goddess of love. Mr. Boyce told us about her during a lesson on Greek mythology, but in Greece she's called Aphrodite. He said the Romans stole all the Greek gods and gave them new Latin names but didn't change their psychopathic personalities. No matter what you call her, he said, Venus caused trouble in Greece and Italy and anywhere else she went.

Mr. Boyce said that love is a game to Venus. She entertains herself by making people fall in love with each other, and then she makes one of them stop loving the other one, and the trouble begins.

Venus has already messed up my imaginary romance with Rob. I don't want her to ruin anything else. Not because I believe in an ancient goddess often seen without her arms, but because love really does go bad sometimes.

6

Skylar and I go to the pool three days in a row without seeing Mr. Boyce. Skylar says it's because his wife doesn't want us hanging around him. She's probably right, but I don't understand why Mrs. Boyce feels that way about us. He's our favorite teacher. You'd think she'd be glad her husband is so popular with his students.

On Monday it rains again, and we spend the day reading.

I finish *Never Let Me Go*, but it's not the sort of book that leaves you feeling happy. I didn't see the big surprise coming. It was definitely not something you'd tell someone who hasn't read the book.

The next day, Skylar and I go to the library to choose another book from the list. This time I want to pick one that ends happily. My hand lingers on *The Yearling*. The fawn on the cover reminds me of the dead deer in the woods, and I look for something else. I finally settle on *The Red Pony.*

Skylar chooses the same book because she loves horses. When we were nine, we spent a whole summer galloping instead of running. When no one was around, we whinnied. We were wild horses, and no one would ever tame us, Skylar said.

In real life, the closest we've gotten to a horse is taking riding lessons for a Girl Scout badge. I got the worst horse of all. He didn't do a thing I said, and then he ran all the way back to the barn with me hanging on like a terrified monkey or something. That was the end of the horse badge for me.

We settle down in Skylar's living room and read. The rain falls softly, no thunder, no lightning. It drips from trees and the eaves and gurgles in the downspouts. Ms. Freeman microwaves popcorn for us, something Mom would never do, because we'd spill it everywhere and besides, it has no nutritional value. You might as well eat Styrofoam, she says.

Luckily, Ms. Freeman's mind does not work the same way. How she and Mom remain friends is just another one of life's mysteries.

It's still raining on Wednesday, so we go to the mall and hang out in the food court with Lindsey, Nessa, and

Erica for a while. Jonathon and his friend Nate come along and sit down with us. I notice that Jonathon looks at Skylar when she's looking at someone else, as if he doesn't want her to catch him staring. I'm pretty sure that means he likes her, especially when he starts getting straws and blowing the paper wrappers at her. She gets all flustered and acts like he's really annoying, but I can tell she's secretly enjoying it.

The boys leave for soccer practice. Rain or shine, their coach says. Lindsey, Nessa, and Erica drift away to browse in the Gap. Skylar and I take the glass elevator to the next level. We stop in front of the Super Palace Nine and look at the signs over the ticket booths. Nothing is showing that we want to see, even if we could afford it. Car chases, superheroes, psycho killers, and Disney.

We amble along, staring in store windows and picking out things we might buy someday. For instance, there's a big red couch in the Sofa Store, the kind that's so soft and plushy, once you sink into it, you never want to get up.

"Someday we'll have houses of our own," Skylar says, "and we'll have matching red couches like that one. When we visit each other, we'll sit on them and remember things we did when we were kids."

It's hard to imagine having a house of my own, but I go along with Skylar and the red sofas.

Next we stop at Victoria's Secret and look at the sexy underwear. "Which bra would you buy?" Skylar asks.

I choose a shocking pink one made of see-through lace, and Skylar picks the same one in black. They both have push-up cups. We whoop with laughter, trying to imagine ourselves parading around in the bras and matching thongs.

Still laughing, Skylar says, "Remember when we dressed up in Mom's sexy date outfits and took pictures?"

I lean against the store window, hiccupping with giggles. "I've still got those photos on my phone."

"Get rid of them!" Skylar says.

"No way. I plan to blackmail you with them."

Just as we're calming down, my art teacher walks out of the shop carrying a Victoria's Secret bag along with an even bigger Macy's bag. Ms. Sullivan is my favorite teacher after Mr. Boyce. She's young and pretty and just started this year. She's had a hard time with rowdy kids in some of her classes, but not ours. We all want good grades, even in art, which is only half a credit.

Even though I'm glad to see Ms. Sullivan, it's kind of weird to catch her coming out of Victoria's Secret. She's my teacher. I don't want to know she wears lacy bras or sexy lingerie. Isn't that why the store has *Secret* in its name? Like nobody should know what's under your clothes?

When I say hello, she looks at me like I'm a stranger. Maybe she's embarrassed too.

"It's me, Abbi."

She smiles and juggles her bags to give me a one-armed hug. "Abbi, I'm so sorry. I was lost in thought," she says. "How are you? How's your summer going?"

"Okay," I say. "Kind of boring and hot, though."

"The end-of-summer blues. Teachers get them, too, you know." She smiles again, but she seems kind of flustered. She probably wishes she'd met me at Macy's instead of here.

"Are you keeping up with your drawing?" she asks.

"Not as much as I should, but I'm really looking forward to art when school starts."

"And I'm looking forward to teaching you!" She glances at Skylar, who is standing there waiting for me to introduce her.

"This is Skylar," I say. "She takes music instead of art. Maybe you saw her in *Bye Bye Birdie*? She sang the lead, and she was so good. Ms. Woodley says Skylar's her best student ever." I realize I'm talking too much, something I do when I'm nervous. I must be picking up Ms. Sullivan's mood.

"Oh, yes, of course," Ms. Sullivan says. "The seventh-grade musical. You were marvelous, Skylar. Everyone was so impressed."

"Thank you." Skylar blushes. "It was lots of fun. I'm trying out next year, too. And I'm already in chorus."

Ms. Sullivan shifts her bags from one hand to the other. "I'd love to hear more about your summer, girls, but I have an appointment at four, and it's already past three."

We say goodbye and watch her walk away. She turns and calls, "Have a great summer, you two—what's left of it, that is. See you when school starts." She turns again and leaves the mall.

"She's so nice," I say. "And she's a really good artist. I've learned a lot from her."

"I wonder what she bought in Victoria's Secret." Skylar giggles and nudges me. "Maybe that sexy black bra I liked. And the matching thong."

I pull away, mortified. "It's none of our business what she bought."

"Don't be so uptight, Abbi. My mom buys lots of stuff there. Where do you think she got the sexy things we wore when we took those pictures?"

"I'm not uptight. I just never thought about Ms. Sullivan going there. It surprised me, that's all."

While we're walking, I try to imagine my mother in Victoria's Secret. Ms. Freeman, yes; my mom, no. Her underwear comes from Macy's. No secret there. I see it in the laundry.

Skylar stops to look at a pair of jeans in Nordstrom's. "One hundred and eighty-five dollars," she says. "That's crazy. They look just like jeans in the Gap at half the price."

We go into Starbucks and order mocha Frappuccinos with whipped cream. Once again, we both spend what's left of our allowances. We need to do some serious babysitting.

It's stopped raining, so we sit at a table outside where we can see Ms. Freeman when she comes to pick us up.

Skylar takes a big slurp of Frappuccino and leans toward me. In a low voice she asks, "Do you think Jonathon likes me?"

"Are you kidding? He's madly in love with you!"

"I'm serious."

"So am I. He kept sneaking looks at you, and then he blew those wrappers in your face. True love, Skylar."

Her face turns red, and she laughs like she can't stop, and then I laugh too. We must be crazy or something. Everything sets us off. First Victoria's Secret and now Jonathon.

When we finally get serious again, Skylar says, "He's really cute, isn't he? The way his hair falls in his face and he flips it out of his eyes. I like him so much. I hope you're right about him liking me."

I look at her and can't believe she's worried about

Jonathon liking her. "Of course I'm right," I tell her. "You're totally beautiful."

If her mother hadn't arrived just then, we would have had another laughing fit.

The sun is out on Thursday, so we go to the tree house to watch the cars come and go. It's already hot when we leave. And even more humid. It's like the trees and mud puddles are breathing water into the air.

"I hope they come today," I say.

"What if they stop meeting there?" Skylar asks. "We'll never figure out who they are or what they're doing."

"If only we were old enough to drive," I say, "we could follow them."

"If we were old enough to drive," Skylar says, "we'd be at the beach on a day like this."

"It must be magic to go wherever you like," I say.

"After we graduate from high school," Skylar says, her voice dreamy, "we'll get a car and drive all the way across the country to the Pacific Ocean."

By the time we come to the end of Marie Drive, we've planned the whole trip, including stops at the Grand Canyon, Death Valley, and Yellowstone. We'll camp in a tent to save money, but every now and then we'll splurge and stay in a fancy motel with a swimming pool and a gym and free breakfast. Our room will have two king-size beds, a walk-in shower with glass doors, and a huge wide-screen TV. Neither one of us has ever stayed in a motel like this, but we've seen commercials.

In the tree house, we open our books, but neither of us likes the way the story is going. We're both afraid something bad is going to happen to the pony. Foreshadowing is what Mr. Boyce calls it when the author throws out hints about the future. We can't say we haven't been warned.

Skylar wants to skip ahead and see if the pony is still alive at the end. If it's not, she says she won't read the rest. She'll start another book. *Artemis Fowl* maybe. That's what Jonathon's reading. He loves it.

I'm tempted to do the same. It's weird. I don't care when a writer kills a human character—unless it's a character I really like, such as Beth in *Little Women*. I still hate Louisa May Alcott for killing Beth off when there was no real reason to do it. But if an animal dies, like *Old Yeller*, that's it for me. I'll never read another one of that writer's books.

After a while, the SUV parks under the tree house. If only the man would get out and we could see him. If only the woman would arrive without the hat and sunglasses. I really want to know what they look like.

Usually the gray car and the SUV arrive around the same time. This time at least five minutes go by before the gray car pulls up behind the SUV.

Is this important? Maybe. I write it down in a note-book, which also contains my reading notes. I take a picture, too.

The mystery woman gets out and slams her door, also unusual enough to make a note of. Today she's wearing her hat and sunglasses, but she's got on a cute sundress with little blue flowers printed all over it. I've never seen her so dressed up. Maybe this is a special occasion and she wants to look really good.

I take a couple of pictures before she gets into the SUV and closes its door with another bang. They don't leave right away. Pretty soon, their voices rise. We can't hear the words, but they're definitely arguing.

"Uh-oh," Skylar mutters. "Sounds like a fight."

I never understand half of what goes on between Mom and Greg when they're cross with each other—funny looks sometimes, silences other times. It's like they argue in a code I can't crack. But the mystery couple doesn't bother hiding their anger.

Skylar and I lean out of the tree house and listen. The car windows are closed, so we can't hear what they're fighting about.

"Maybe he's mad at her for being late," I say.

Skylar shakes her head. "It's more than that."

"Maybe one of their assassinations went wrong and

their controller is sending them back to Russia," I say. "He wants to go, she doesn't."

"Maybe you should write a spy novel," Skylar says. "You're really good at making up stuff."

"What do you mean?"

"Come on, Abbi, they're not spies. That's kid stuff. They're cheaters, sneaking around on the people they're married to. Like my dad and the woman he ran off with."

"Come on, Skylar," I say. "Not everybody's like your dad."

She gives me a look that clearly says I don't know what goes on in parked cars. "Face it, Abbi, it makes a lot more sense than imagining they're spies."

The detective game collapses. I see it for what it is, a game for kids like Skylar and me back in the days of our first tree house and Nancy Drew and all that. The only mystery here is who the people are and why they meet at the dead end of Marie Drive in the worst part of Evansburg.

But still, I'm sad to let the spy theory go. It's like we're losing something, Skylar and me.

The SUV's passenger door flies open and the woman practically jumps out. The man says something in a low, angry voice. She shouts, "Leave me alone!"

Instead of getting into her car, she sets out across the field toward the woods. She takes short, fast steps, her shoulders tense, the way people walk when they're mad. I video her until she's a dot on the screen, too small to identify.

I expect the man to run after her, but he just sits in the SUV. He doesn't even call after her. Maybe he thinks she'll see that she's wrong and come back. Suddenly he starts the SUV, does a U-turn, and drives away so fast the tires spray dust and gravel.

"He's really mad," Skylar whispers.

"So is she. It must have been a major fight."

"Let's follow her, make sure she's okay. He might have hit her or something." Skylar scoots down the tree, with me close behind her. We run after the woman, but before we're halfway across the field, she disappears into the woods.

We stop to catch our breath. "What should we do?" I ask Skylar. "She might not like us coming after her, asking what's wrong and is she all right. She doesn't even know us—she might think we're nosy, like it's none of our business."

Skylar pushes her hair out of her face. "Maybe she needs to be by herself till she calms down. That's how I'd feel if I just had a big fight with my boyfriend."

We walk back across the field, slower now, feeling the heat. We look in the gray car's side window. The pink hoodie lies on the seat just like before. The yoga bag is on the floor behind the driver's seat. The art book is gone.

"She didn't take her phone," Skylar says. "Or her purse."

Sure enough, the phone's in plain sight on the console between the front seats, and the purse is on the floor on the passenger side.

"That's weird," I say. "She always takes her purse when she gets in the SUV."

"Maybe she was too mad to think about anything but having it out with him," Skylar says. "Maybe she was going to break up with him if he didn't leave his wife and marry her. She could even be pregnant."

I don't like Skylar's story, but she knows much more about cheating husbands than I do.

"She shouldn't have fallen for a married man," Skylar says.

"But Skylar, we don't know for sure he's married."

"Trust me. He's married. And he's a cheater."

She's made up her mind. It's no use arguing. It's her story, not mine.

Skylar tries the car's door. It's locked. She peers in the window again. "That's the latest iPhone, and she's left it in plain sight. They cost a fortune. I want one for my birthday, but I might as well ask for a trip to the moon."

We stare longingly at the phone and purse. All our

answers are a few inches away on the other side of a closed window. For a second, I think about picking up a stone and smashing the glass. I have a feeling Skylar's thinking the same thing. But neither of us does it.

"Why did she run into the woods?" I ask. "Why didn't she just drive home?"

"She probably expected him to come after her," Skylar says. "They'd make up, and everything would be fine. If she drove home, it would be the end of it. Women do that a lot in movies. Sometimes it works— but not always."

I look at the woods, dark and still on the other side of the field. Crows call. A breeze moves through the weeds like waves. I think of the dead deer and the bullet holes in the Private Property sign. I think of Carter and Jason and the drugs. In the movies Skylar mentioned, the woman who runs into the woods usually turns up dead. All of a sudden I'm sure the woman in the flowered dress is not coming back.

Skylar reads my mind. "You think something's wrong."

"Don't you?"

"You're the one who gets feelings about things." She stares across the field. A cloud drifts in front of the sun and the woods darken. The wind makes bigger waves in the weeds. "She's probably walking to town along the railroad tracks right now. She'll call the man and they'll make up."

"How can she call him?" I ask. "She didn't take her phone."

"There's a pay phone at the Food Lion."

"Except she left her purse in the car."

"Stop worrying, Abbi," Skylar says. "We'll come back tomorrow and her car will be gone and you'll feel silly for thinking the worst."

Skylar starts walking toward the tree house. No matter what she says, I still have a bad feeling about the woman in the flowered dress. The woods—she shouldn't have gone there. She should have gotten in her car and driven home where she'd be safe.

We're not in the mood to stay, so we get our stuff together to go home. Skylar's halfway down the ladder and I'm right behind her when Jason and Carter appear. They're riding their fancy new bikes, but when they see us, they dump them and head toward the tree.

"You dogs are spying on us," Carter yells.

They're at the bottom of the tree now, staring up at us. This is all we need. I want to go home. I've had enough of the tree house and the cars and even Skylar. She probably feels exactly the same way.

Before we know what he's doing, Jason pushes past Skylar on the ladder. On the way up, he grabs my backpack. I lose my grip and fall, not far enough to kill me, but it hurts when I land hard on my butt.

Carter shoves Skylar out of his way and takes her backpack. She doesn't fall but loses her footing and sort of slides down the trunk, grabbing at the steps as she goes and skinning her knees.

The two of us scramble to our feet. It's no use climbing up after them. They'll just push us off.

"Give us our packs," Skylar shouts.

"Come and get them," Carter says. Jason laughs.

They dump stuff out of our backpacks onto the platform and paw through it.

"Hey, Carter, look at this." Jason holds up my book. "They know how to read."

He says *read* like it's some weird, perverted thing. He tears pages from the book and tosses them into the air. We watch fragments from the story fall into the weeds.

"Stop it," Skylar shouts. "Those are library books!"

Carter laughs. "You're gonna pay for them, not us."

Jason reads a sentence out loud. His voice jerks and sputters, and I wonder if he really reads that badly or if he's just pretending. "What a dumb title. Who ever heard of a red pony?"

After they've destroyed both books, they find our water bottles and empty them on our heads.

"You dogs get out of here or we'll take your cheap

bikes, too," Carter says in that sneering voice of his. "You got no idea how much trouble you'll be in if you keep coming here and messing with us."

"This tree house is ours now," Jason yells. They laugh.

"You think you're so smart," Skylar yells back, kicking one of the bikes. "But we know how you got these fancy bikes."

I pull her away. "Shut up, you're just making things worse!"

She ignores me. "If you don't give us our backpacks, we'll—"

"You'll what?"

"Come on," I beg her. "Let's get out of here!"

Skylar gives Carter and Jason a long, hard look. Before she can say anything else, I whisper, "Don't mention drugs. You'll get Rob in trouble."

We yank our bikes out of the weeds. Jason throws our empty backpacks at us. Mine hits my shoulder and knocks me off my bike.

Carter yells, "I better not see you here again!" They both laugh some more.

We ride away without looking back.

7

When we are safe, we stop in the middle of our street, halfway between my house and Skylar's. We're almost too exhausted to talk.

"No more tree house," I say.

Skylar wipes the sweat out of her eyes. "I'm done with it anyway."

A kid coasts past on his skateboard. The little girls next door draw chalk stick figures on the sidewalk. Mrs. Goetz walks past with her dog, Silky. She smiles and waves at us.

It's like a picture in a children's book, one of those illustrations where the artist hides things for you to find. Secret things. Scary things. Things you won't notice if you don't look closely.

Mom's car turns the corner. She sees us and stops. "What are you doing in the middle of the street?"

I say goodbye to Skylar and pedal down the driveway behind the car. After Mom turns off the engine, I park my bike where it belongs.

The next day, we meet Lindsey, Nessa, and Erica at the swimming pool. Mrs. Boyce is there with Andy Junior. She looks mad and sad at the same time. We wonder where Mr. Boyce is, but we aren't about to ask. She'd bite our heads off.

"He was with her yesterday," Nessa says. "But they didn't stay long. We barely said hi before they left. The baby was crying, and she looked mad as usual."

"Maybe he'll come later," Skylar says.

"I keep telling you guys they're getting a divorce," Erica says. "My mom's been divorced twice. Believe me, I know the signs."

Lindsey rubs sunscreen on her nose. "Every divorce is different—that's what my mom says. Sometimes people think a marriage is perfect, but then it's not after all. Sometimes people fight all the time, and everyone thinks they'll get a divorce, but they never do."

We all stare at Mrs. Boyce. She's sitting in the wading pool with Andy, but it's like she's not really there. She's definitely not happy.

"I don't understand," says Nessa. "Mr. Boyce is so cute and so nice and so smart. How could anyone be unhappy or cross with him?"

None of us has the answer.

When Jonathon and some other guys show up, we forget about Mr. Boyce. They cannonball into the pool and mess around ducking each other. We jump into the pool near them, and Jonathon ducks Skylar. She comes up laughing and spluttering and tries to duck him. He swims away underwater. The next thing I know, he's jumping off the high board. He and his friends horse around in the deep end, but I get out of the pool. I'm not that great a swimmer, and I'm nervous in water over my head.

I glance at the wading pool, hoping to see Mr. Boyce. He's not there, and neither is Mrs. Boyce. The little yellow duck is bobbing around in the water. I rescue it, thinking I can give it to Andy the next time I see him. Hopefully, Mr. Boyce will be here, and he'll say I'm even more super-duper than he thought.

It rains the next day and the day after that. We go to the mall, we go to the library and pay fines for our ruined books. The library's other copies are checked out, so we go to the used bookstore and buy beat-up paperbacks of *The Red Pony*.

It turns out to be the biggest waste of money ever because in the end, the boy has to shoot the pony, which is the most horrible thing I've ever read. Think what it would be like to Kill. Your. Own. Pony. Mr. Boyce would probably say it's supposed to be a big life lesson of some kind, but I will never read another book by John Steinbeck, and neither will Skylar. We are done with him.

After dinner, Mom watches the local news while I load the dishwasher.

"Abbi," she calls, "don't you have a teacher named Sullivan?"

"She's my art teacher. Why?"

"The *News at Seven* has just announced that she's missing."

I look at the TV in time to see Ms. Sullivan's face on the screen. I freeze as the newswoman says, "If you have any information, please call the police at this number."

When a shampoo commercial with happy music comes on, Mom turns off the TV.

I drop down on the sofa beside her. "What happened?"

"Her sister had been trying to call her, but it went straight to voice mail. When Ms. Sullivan didn't return her calls, her sister went to her apartment. She wasn't there, and neither was her car. So she called the police."

I'm getting scared. It sounds wrong somehow, another story that won't end well.

"She's only been gone a couple of days," Mom says,

putting her arm around me and drawing me closer. "Maybe she decided to take a little trip. People do that."

"But why didn't she tell her sister?"

"Don't worry, Abbi. I'm sure Ms. Sullivan will be home soon."

I hope she's right, but even after I go to bed, I worry. Mom knows that things upset me, she knows how my mind always goes to the worst thing, so she tries to show me the positive side of everything. Ms. Sullivan is fine; nothing's happened to her. But still, I worry.

The next day, Ms. Sullivan is still missing. The morning news people speculate about foul play, an expression I hate—it's so creepy and horrible and sends my mind reeling to dark places.

Mom turns off the TV. "Don't pay attention," she says. "They always exaggerate. The police are still calling it a missing person case."

After Mom leaves for work, Skylar comes over and we sit on the porch steps and talk about Ms. Sullivan.

"She was worried about something when we saw her at the mall," I say.

"She didn't look worried to me," Skylar says. "Remember her shopping bags? Maybe she bought new clothes for a trip and she's in New York City. Isn't that where artists hang out?"

"She'd tell her sister if she was going away."

"You don't know what she does when she's not teaching. She might have a whole secret life."

I lean back on my elbows. Skylar's right. I don't know anything about Ms. Sullivan's private life. I make up stories about her, about her apartment and her furniture and why she isn't married, but all I really know is what she's like in school.

"One thing I do know about her—she loves hiking," I tell Skylar. "Remember that story in the news last year about the woman who fell off a cliff in California?"

"The one who landed on a beach, and nobody could see her from the road?"

"She was there for three or four days, maybe a week, trying to catch somebody's attention. Finally this couple came along with their dog and she was rescued."

"So why are you telling me this?" Skylar asks.

"Because Ms. Sullivan could have gone hiking in a state park and fallen down a cliff and they'll find her alive and okay, just like the woman in California."

While I talk, I picture Ms. Sullivan in her hiking boots, trapped at the bottom of a cliff. Maybe she broke her arm or her leg and she can't climb out and there's no signal for her phone. At last, these people come along and their dog smells her and she's rescued. I see it clearly on *News at Seven*, the big story of the day. The more I make up, the more real my story gets.

Skylar stands up and stretches. "That could be," she

says. "Yeah, she might have done that."

She looks at me. "What do you want to do today?"

"I don't know. What do you want to do?"

"I asked first."

We laugh because we've been having this conversation since third grade. Skylar usually ends up being the one to pick.

"Let's ride our bikes to Marie Drive and see if the car's still there," she says.

When I hesitate, she says, "Come on, Abbi. I know you want to."

She's right. I've been worrying about the car. If it's gone, I'll know the woman came back and drove away and I can stop worrying about her.

Keeping an eye out for Jason and Carter, we pedal down Marie Drive.

Gnats swarm around my face. Sweat runs down my back. If we'd gone to the pool, we'd be up to our chins in water now. Jonathon might be showing off on the diving board. Mr. Boyce might be at the wading pool with Andy. Maybe Mrs. Boyce stayed home to clean the house or something, and Skylar and I could talk to him without her frowning at us and making him leave early.

We come to the end of Marie Drive without seeing Jason or Carter. But the gray car is still where the woman left it. Parked slightly crooked, its front tires off the road, dappled by the shade of our tree.

The sight of it sends a shiver up my spine. Why hasn't she come back for it?

Skylar grabs my arm. "Somebody broke the side window."

We go closer, pedaling slowly, cautiously. Bright bits of safety glass glitter in the weeds. We lay our bikes down and peer through the broken window. More safety glass is scattered across the seat and the dashboard. The phone is gone. So is the purse.

"Jason and Carter," Skylar mutters. "What do you want to bet?"

I take pictures of the broken window and the bits of glass. My heart thumps. I'm collecting evidence of a real crime now.

"What if this is Ms. Sullivan's car?" Skylar asks.

"What?" I stare at her. "No way. She couldn't possibly be the woman who owns this car. Ms. Sullivan wouldn't—"

"How can there be two missing women in Evansburg at the same time, but we only hear about one on the news?"

"Maybe the woman who owns this car isn't missing."

"Then where is she?" Skylar asks. "Why is her car still here?"

"Oh, my God." I sit down in the dust beside the car.

I don't want it to belong to Ms. Sullivan. I don't want her to be the woman who met a man here. I don't want her to be the woman in the flowered sundress who went into the woods and never came back.

"But the man," I whisper. "Who was the man in the SUV?"

"Some loser who didn't care what happened to her," Skylar says. "A cheater like my dad."

"What should we do?"

"What do you mean? What can we do?"

"Tell the police where her car is?"

"And get in big-time trouble with our mothers?" Skylar frowns. "We don't know for absolutely sure it's Ms. Sullivan's car. Maybe I'm wrong. Maybe the mystery woman isn't Ms. Sullivan. We should wait and see what happens."

I get up and brush the dust off my shorts. "Let's go home. I never want to see this place again."

On the way, we pass a Quik Stop. We have just enough change to buy two bottles of water. We sit on the curb near the gas pumps and drink.

We're about to leave when an old red pickup truck stops in front of one of the pumps. The driver gets out, shoves a credit card into the slot, and opens his gas tank. It's the guy from Dairy Queen.

The snakes tattooed on his arms twist and turn

when he moves. His biceps are huge, his shoulders are wide, and he has almost no neck.

He wears those mirrored sunglasses that totally hide your eyes, but I recognize him. "That's Paul," I tell her, "the guy Jason and Carter know."

"He looks like their type, all right."

"It must hurt to get that many tattoos," I whisper.

"Did you know Mom has one?" Skylar whispers back.

I stare at her wide-eyed and shake my head. It's impossible to imagine *my* mother having a tattoo. But Ms. Freeman, yes, I can picture her getting one. Not sleeves like Paul's, though. I would have seen them.

"She has a little butterfly on her shoulder," Skylar says, "small enough to hide under a Band-Aid. She says when I'm eighteen I can get one, but I don't think I will."

We must have talked louder than we thought. Paul lifts his head and looks at us. "Like what you see, girls?"

I feel my face turn red, but Skylar gives him the ugly eye and says, "No, we don't like what we see."

Without looking at him again, we dump our empty bottles in the recycle bin and start to ride away. I wish Skylar hadn't shot her mouth off. This guy is a lot scarier than Carter and Jason.

"Hold it." Suddenly Paul's in front of us, blocking

our way. "You're the two girls who hang out in the tree house, aren't you? Carter told me about you, nosing around. What are you up to?"

Here we are, in the middle of the day, in the Quik Stop parking lot, with cars pulling in and out, people getting gas, buying snacks and sodas, and not one of them paying any attention to Skylar and me. Paul could throw us into his truck and drive away, and none of these people would even notice.

"Buzz off," Skylar yells at him. "We don't talk to strangers."

The man at the closest gas pump looks over at us. His wife points her phone at Paul. The man says, "Are you bothering these girls?"

Everyone's looking now. Paul mutters something and saunters back to his truck, shrugging and smirking like it's all a big nothing. The woman videos him anyway.

Skylar and I jump on our bikes and turn down a side road that leads to our neighborhood. Just to be safe, we hide behind a tall hedge and watch to see if he's following us. No sign of him.

When we think it's safe, we get back on our bikes and ride for home. Lucky for us, it's downhill almost all the way.

Safe in front of our houses, I look at Skylar. I can't

help laughing. "*Buzz off?* Where did that come from?"

"I can't believe I said it." Skylar laughs. "I must've heard it on an old TV show or something. I opened my mouth, and out it came."

We both laugh, kind of hysterically. I feel like we escaped a huge danger, but I don't know what it was. Like a cloud passing in front of the sun, dark for a moment, then light again. But I'm glad the woman was there and ready to video our kidnapping, if that's what Paul was planning.

That night, Greg comes over. After dinner, we watch the local news. Ms. Sullivan is still missing. The police have interviewed all the teachers. Several of them have agreed to talk to a reporter, including Mr. Boyce. Mom met him at PTA, of course, but I point him out to Greg.

"So that's the guy you're always quoting," he says. "Good-looking chap."

I blush, and Greg laughs.

"He's the best language arts teacher I've ever had. You should hear him read poetry. He makes it come to life like a song written yesterday or something." I thump my heart. "I feel the words right here."

"For me, it was my baseball coach," Greg says. "He never recited any poems, but he taught me a lot about being a good sport and trying my hardest and all that."

"I wish Mr. Boyce could be my teacher every year. I'll miss his class so much when school starts." With a sigh, I settle back on the couch between Greg and Mom. When it's Mr. Boyce's turn to speak, I lean forward and stare at his face. He looks sad and tired and worried.

"We all love Kris," he says. "She's a joy to work with. Caring, compassionate, fantastic sense of humor, always willing to listen or to pitch in and help. The students are crazy about her, even the ones who usually hate art."

He takes a deep breath, and his face saddens the way it does when he reads certain poems. "Please, Kris, come back to us."

Mr. Boyce has shadows under his eyes, like he isn't sleeping. My heart is breaking for him.

The newswoman turns to Mr. Herman, my algebra teacher. It's weird to see him and the rest of the faculty on TV. They're gathered around a table in the newsroom. Behind them is a blown-up picture of Ms. Sullivan, taken on a day when she never expected to be a missing person.

Our principal, Ms. Greenbaum, winds things up. "We all hope Ms. Sullivan will return safely. She's an outstanding member of our faculty, a great art teacher, and an award-winning artist herself." She stares into the camera. "We love you, Kris. Be safe and come back to us."

The newscaster brings the show to a close, and a Pepsi commercial comes on.

"When they show ads like that after a serious program," Mom says, "it trivializes everything—as if they're saying that a soda and Ms. Sullivan are equally important."

Greg gives Mom a hug, then turns off the TV and says, "How about a trip to Dairy Queen? We need some cheering up."

"Can Skylar come with us?" I ask.

"Of course," Mom says.

I text her, and she meets us at the truck, ready to go. We climb into the small seat behind Greg and Mom.

"Did you watch the news?" she asks me.

"Mr. Boyce looked so sad."

"I felt sorry for him, didn't you?"

"I did. He's so sensitive."

"It's the poetry," Skylar says. "Every poem we read this year was sad."

There's a big crowd at the DQ, and Greg offers to stand in line for all of us. We grab a picnic table and wait for our shakes.

All around us the cicadas are singing in the treetops and the lightning bugs are flickering on and off like little sparks in the dark. The line moves slowly. People laugh and talk. A baby cries. Traffic whizzes back and forth on Route 203.

Sometimes we hear a radio blast part of a song before the car speeds away. Skylar and I try to guess what it is. Mom shouts out "the Rolling Stones," and we laugh and say you have to be really old to recognize them.

At last Greg comes back with our order. Just as we finish up, we hear sirens, lots of them. Like a parade, but much faster, fire engines, ambulances, and police cars streak past. Lights flash blue and red across our faces. The sight of so many emergency vehicles scares me. Something awful has happened. People are hurt, dying. My throat clogs, and I push away what's left of my shake.

"Must be a bad accident," Greg says.

"I'm surprised it doesn't happen more often," Mom says. "People drive way too fast on Route 203."

Skylar looks at me. "What's wrong?"

"Nothing." I shrug. "I just hate the sound of all those sirens."

"You've got a bad feeling," she says. "I can tell by the look on your face."

Greg gets up and collects our trash. Mom puts her hand on my arm. "This has nothing to do with Ms. Sullivan, if that's what you're thinking."

"Maybe they found her." Skylar says it like it's bad news. Not good—like she's alive and well.

I try to keep my mind from going there, but of course she's right. Bad news is exactly what I'm thinking. The worst, the very worst. My heart speeds up. I feel dizzy.

Greg comes back from the trash can and jingles his keys. The mood at DQ has changed. People are heading for their cars. The baby starts to cry again.

We get into the truck. "Can Skylar sleep over?" I ask.

"If it's okay with her mother," Mom says.

When we get home, Skylar runs to her house and comes back with pajamas and a toothbrush. We go to my room and close the door.

"It's sure to be on *News at Eleven*," Skylar says.

I look at my iPad. "It's only a little after ten now."

We put on our pajamas and brush our teeth. That takes less than five minutes.

Skylar goes to my window. "It's so odd to look at my house from your house. I can see Pot Head watching TV. It's like he's a doll in a doll's house."

The front door opens below us. Mom tells Greg good night. He gives her a hug and a kiss and says not to forget that they have a dinner date Friday. "At my place."

Mom stands on the front steps and watches Greg drive away. When the taillights are out of sight, she comes inside.

"Why don't they get married?" Skylar asks.

"It's not Greg—he wants to marry her, he talks about it all the time in a joking way, but she pretends not to hear him. Sometimes I think she's scared he'll turn out like my father and walk out on her."

"Greg? No way. He's crazy about her. My mother would give anything to find a guy like him."

Somewhere in the night we hear sirens again, faint now, far away, just a little louder than the cicadas. Everything we haven't talked about comes rushing back. Ms. Sullivan, the fire engines, ambulances, and police cars we saw on Route 203.

We turn out the light and get into bed so Mom will think we're asleep. Otherwise, she'll come in and talk for a while. We want to watch *News at Eleven* on our own. My iPad's glow lights our faces and some of my room. Everything else is dark. The news begins with a close-up of the reporter's face. "I am sad to announce," she says, "that the body of Kristina Sullivan was found this evening in a wooded area near the end of Marie Drive."

I grab Skylar's hand, not believing what we've just heard. It's like a car crash in my brain. It can't be true. There must be a mistake.

"No," I whisper. "No, please no. NO! NO! NO!"

The reporter keeps talking. "The police have issued no further details, but we expect a full report tomorrow. In the meantime, our thoughts and prayers are with Ms. Sullivan's family and friends. We mourn the tragic death of a young and brilliant teacher."

Skylar and I cry and hold each other tight.

"I can't believe it," Skylar says, sobbing. "It's not right. It's not fair."

A policewoman appears on the screen. She talks about Ms. Sullivan's car, which is missing. She shows another photograph. In this one Ms. Sullivan stands beside a small gray car, her hand on the hood, smiling into the camera.

"It's a gray 2005 Honda Civic," the officer says, "Maryland plates, 3MB5098."

Skylar gasps. "Oh my God, I was right. It is Ms. Sullivan's car. It was her we saw, your teacher, I can't believe it."

I sit beside her like I've gone catatonic, can't move, can't speak. I can hardly breathe. I didn't hear what I just heard, I didn't see what I just saw. It just won't sink into my brain.

The number matches the license plate in my pictures.

The policewoman is still talking, but her voice seems muffled, far away, hard to hear. "If you have any

information about this car, contact the police immediately. It's essential to our investigation."

Skylar grabs my arm, shakes me. "Abbi, we've got
to tell the police about the car and the SUV. What if
they don't know that Ms. Sullivan was meeting a man
in secret?"

I stare at my iPad, holding it so tightly my fingers
turn white. Skylar sounds far away too. Her words are
meaningless.

She tightens her grip on my arm. Her fingernails
press into my skin. "Listen to me, Abbi. We have to tell
the police!"

I wince and pull away from her. She's right, we have
to tell the police, but what about Mom? She'll find out,
she'll be so angry. I can't, I can't . . .

Finally I find my voice. "Our mothers will find out
where we've been, what we've been doing. They'll be so
mad."

"What's more important, Abbi? Helping the police
find your teacher's killer or not getting in trouble with
your mother?"

I think about Ms. Sullivan and how much she
encouraged me, how special she made me feel. If there's
anything I can do to solve her murder, I have to do it,
no matter what happens.

"Okay, you're right. We'll go to the police, but how? I

mean, do we walk into the police station and tell them? Or do we call them or—what should we do?" The only policeman I've ever spoken to is Officer Bob, who came to our school for Safety Day in fourth grade.

Skylar chews on her fingernail. "Maybe we should talk to somebody first. Greg, maybe."

"The first thing he'd do is tell Mom."

"Who else can we trust?"

"How about Mr. Boyce? He'll know what to do. Maybe he'd even go to the station with us."

"You're a genius, Abbi." Skylar hugs me. "We'll call him tomorrow morning."

I start crying again. Skylar tries to comfort me, but I can't stop. This is the most horrible night of my life. I can't imagine what tomorrow will be like. And all the days after, plodding past in a long gray line. I press my face into my pillow and sob until my eyes hurt.

Skylar lies beside me, her body spooned around mine, her arms holding me. Slowly her grip relaxes. Her breath is deep and even. She's sound asleep.

Even though I'm more tired than I've ever been in my life, I can't relax. Over and over again, I see Ms. Sullivan getting into the SUV, her face hidden by sunglasses and that crazy straw hat. I see her coming out of Victoria's Secret with her big shopping bags, I see her jump out of the SUV and walk across the field and

disappear into the woods. Skylar and I should have followed her. We might have saved her.

But no, we let her go. And so did the man in the
SUV. He drove off and left her, as if he didn't care what
happened to her.

I try to sleep, but my mind just won't let go of Ms.
Sullivan and the man and the police. I toss and turn.
Skylar flops to her other side, her back to me. She's not
awake, but I'm obviously disturbing her sleep.

I slide quietly out of bed. Skylar doesn't move or
make a sound. Nothing wakes her up.

I sit by my window. The trees are dark shapes
against the night sky. The cicadas have sung themselves
to sleep. The only sound is a breeze rustling the leaves.
The only light comes from a streetlamp down the road.

A car drives past. Its headlights sweep across my
ceiling and change all the shadows.

Mrs. Doyle's black cat Pixy glides across the street
like a shadow of itself. What's it like to be a cat, I wonder, and prowl through the dark like you belong there?

After Pixy disappears into a neighbor's shrubbery,
I stay at the window. Everything looks different in the
moonlight—mostly black and white blended together
in blurry shapes. Sharp edges are gone. Shadows trick
your eyes. It's hard to see clearly.

I want to stop thinking, turn off my mind, go to

sleep. Most of all, I want to wake up tomorrow in some other universe, where Skylar and I never rode our bikes down Marie Drive. We never found the tree house or spied on anyone. Ms. Sullivan isn't dead. She'll be my teacher in the fall.

I hold this thought in my head and crawl into bed. Skylar is still asleep, her face peaceful. For now she's not thinking about murder and death. I match my breathing to hers. Deep, slow breaths. Gradually I drift into sleep.

8

While Skylar and I pick at the breakfast Mom fixed for us, an update from the police interrupts the morning weather report. A man with a serious face leans across the news desk and stares into the camera. "In a meeting with the press this morning," he says, "the police chief has provided more details about the murder of Kristina Sullivan, a twenty-two-year-old art teacher at Everett Stone Middle School. Ms. Sullivan was assaulted and killed in the woods near Marie Drive. A thirteen-year-old boy found her body under a pile of branches and trash near the train tracks. So far the police have no suspects. They're imploring persons with information about Kristina Sullivan or her car to contact the police at this number."

I look at the phone number. I want to call and tell the police what we know, but I can't do it. It's too big, too scary. Maybe I should tell Mom everything. She'd call the police. She'd take Skylar and me to the police station.

Skylar catches my eye and shakes her head. She knows I'm about to break down and tell Mom about the SUV, the argument, Ms. Sullivan running into the woods. I take a deep breath and close my mind tightly around our secret. We'll talk to Mr. Boyce. That's what we agreed to do.

"Will you be all right by yourself today?" Mom asks me. "If you need me, I can call in sick."

"Skylar's here." I sniffle. "I'll be okay."

"Are you sure?"

I nod and try to smile, but my mouth wobbles.

Mom is clearly worried. "Maybe you and Skylar should stay with her mom today."

"Mom, I'm fine. Honest."

"I hate to see you go through this." She hugs me so tight I can hardly breathe. "I know how much you liked Ms. Sullivan. I was so impressed with her at PTA. A lovely woman. And a very talented artist." She kisses the tears on my cheeks and steps back to look at me.

"If you change your mind, call me. I'll come straight home." She goes to the door. "Please stay close to home today. I'll be worried until the killer's in jail."

After the door closes behind Mom, the house is so quiet I can hear the tick of the mantel clock in the living room. I slump on the couch and stare at the wall.

There's nowhere I want to go, nothing I want to do. All I can think of is Ms. Sullivan walking across the field, wearing her pretty dress, her silly straw hat, her dark glasses. My teacher, my teacher. I start crying again.

Skylar sits beside me and puts her arms around me. I rest my head on her shoulder.

"I'm sorry," I tell her. "I just can't stop crying. I liked her so much."

"Even though she wasn't my teacher and I didn't know her like you did, I'm really sad too," Skylar says. "She was so nice at the mall. She even remembered me in *Bye Bye Birdie*."

We hug each other and sit together until I stop crying. Skylar brings me a glass of water and I drink it down in gulps that make me feel sick. "What should we do about Mr. Boyce?" she asks.

"We have to talk to him," I say. "He'll tell us the right thing to do. Then maybe I can stop thinking about it all the time. I'm going crazy."

"Should we just go to his house?" Skylar asks. "Or should we call him first?"

"It would be rude to show up at his house without any warning," I say. It's like hearing my mother's voice come out of my mouth.

We look his number up online, but neither one of us wants to pick up the phone. Kids don't call their teachers. He might be busy or something. He might not understand why we're calling him. He might get mad. His wife might answer.

We probably spend half an hour thinking we should call, then thinking we shouldn't. Finally, we flip a quarter. I lose.

His phone rings once. I hang up and hand the phone to Skylar. "I can't do it. You do it."

She takes the phone and calls again. His phone rings and rings for a long time. There's no way to leave a message.

"Maybe he's at the store or something," I say.

"Let's ride our bikes to his house," Skylar says. "By the time we get there, he might be home."

We get his address the same way we got his phone number and start pedaling. I'm not sure this is a good idea, but we're kind of desperate.

It's a long ride, way out on the other side of the mall in a new part of town. I'd pictured Mr. Boyce living in an old Victorian mansion with a tower on the side, but his house is just as ordinary as the other colonials and split-levels on his block. Except that they all have nice yards and shrubbery.

Mr. Boyce's grass needs cutting, and weeds sprout from cracks in his sidewalk. His bushes have grown tall and shaggy. A kid's red wagon full of rainwater sits under a tree, and a big yellow plastic dump truck lies on its side by the door. It's the saddest house on the street.

Skylar and I hesitate, silently daring each other to ring the doorbell. She gives in and presses hard. We hear it chime inside. My heart is beating so fast I'm afraid I'll faint.

"Maybe no one's home," I whisper, kind of hoping I'm right and we can leave before he sees us. I'm hot and sweaty and tired. We shouldn't be here. It's a mistake to have come.

"Should I ring it again?"

Before she presses the button, the door opens and Mr. Boyce stares at us in surprise. "Skylar and Abbi," he says. "What can I do for you?"

His voice is flat, and he looks tired. If we were selling Girl Scout cookies, he'd say he didn't want any. I back away, ready to jump on my bike and leave.

"It's about Ms. Sullivan. We need your advice." Skylar speaks so fast her words bump into each other. It's like she expects him to slam the door before she gets a chance to finish her sentence.

Mr. Boyce doesn't seem to understand what she's saying. He's wearing long, baggy running shorts and an Everett Stone Middle School T-shirt with a coffee stain down the front. His eyes are bloodshot, his hair uncombed, and he has a sort of shadowy whisker beard. I wonder if he's sick. Mom told me that some people at work have been out with the summer flu. Maybe that's what he has.

Then I remember what he said on the news about Ms. Sullivan and how much he hoped she'd return. He must be as sad as we are. We're definitely invading his privacy. We should leave right now.

I nudge Skylar, but she's focused on telling Mr. Boyce why we're here. "It's about Ms. Sullivan," she says again, louder and slower this time. "We don't know what to do."

"Come in," he says. The curtains are closed in the living room, giving it a strange underwater feeling, and the house is hot and stuffy. In the dim light I see a clutter of books and papers and toys scattered on the floor and the furniture. Why hasn't anyone opened the curtains or cleaned up? Where's Mrs. Boyce? Where's Andy?

"You girls must be heartbroken," Mr. Boyce says. "It's terrible. No one knows what to do. No one expected— We all love Kris. She's, she was . . . so kind, so talented." He breaks off and shakes his head.

He sounds so sad. I start crying again.

He pats my shoulder. "Kris is so proud of you," he says. "You're her best student. You are . . . you were . . . I just can't—" He pulls a used tissue out of his pocket and blows his nose.

I cry harder, and he hands me a box of tissues. I start apologizing for crying, but he says, "It's okay to cry, Abbi, it's okay."

"But why did it happen?" I ask. "Why did she die? She was a good person. Why does God allow bad things to happen to people like her? I don't understand."

Mr. Boyce sighs. "Sometimes there's no explanation for things like this," he says. "Even the greatest philosophers can't tell you. It's the big existential question, isn't it?"

He looks at Skylar and me as if he expects us to understand, but neither of us has any idea what *existential* means. It must be a question without an answer.

I blow my nose and wipe my eyes and gulp a few times. Skylar and I follow him to the kitchen, which is a worse mess than the living room. The garbage can is full, and I can smell leftover Chinese takeout. The recycling bin overflows with beer cans. Dirty dishes cover a lot of the countertop and fill the sink. Flies crawl on a cantaloupe rind on the table.

"Excuse the mess," he says. "My wife's mother is recovering from surgery. Rose and Andy are spending a few days with her. I'm not much good at cleaning up after myself."

"You should see my house," Skylar says. Unlike me, she's beginning to relax. "Nobody in my family is any good at cleaning up either."

He pours a cup of coffee from one of those fancy machines that make all sorts of drinks, even cappuccino. "Do you girls drink coffee? Or would you prefer orange juice or water?"

We choose water, and he hands us cold bottles from the refrigerator. We sit at the counter. Skylar presses her bottle to her forehead before she opens it. The house is stiflingly hot. The air conditioner must be broken. I can't get over the feeling we shouldn't be here.

Mr. Boyce turns his sad eyes to us. "Now, what can I help you with?"

"Well, it's kind of a long story," Skylar begins, "but a few weeks ago, Abbi and I found this old tree house down at the end of Marie Drive."

Mr. Boyce drinks his coffee. His hand shakes, and I wish I could comfort him. Instead, I say, "It's a dead-end street way out on the edge of town. What Mom calls the bad side."

Mr. Boyce peers into his coffee cup, his shoulders hunched. He doesn't say anything, he doesn't ask questions. He doesn't even look at us. He just waits for us to go on.

"We were reading the books on our summer list," Skylar says, "and we saw these cars. A black SUV came first and then a gray Honda. A woman got in the man's SUV, and they drove away together. They met there every Thursday and parked right under our tree house."

"We didn't know it then, but the woman who drove

the Honda was Ms. Sullivan," I tell him. "She always wore a disguise—a big straw hat and humongous black glasses." I'm getting tearful again, so I let Skylar take over.

"We never saw the man at all," she says. "He stayed in the SUV."

Mr. Boyce sips his coffee and then stares into the cup as if he expects to read his fortune there. He still hasn't asked a question or looked at either one of us.

"Then, last Thursday, they had a big argument," Skylar says. Her voice rises, as if she's afraid Mr. Boyce isn't listening. "Ms. Sullivan got out and walked across the field into the woods. He didn't go after her. He just let her go and then drove away."

Skylar takes a deep breath like she has to force herself to go on. "We think the man in the SUV killed her."

Mr. Boyce draws in his breath and stares at her as if he can't believe what she's just said. He looks like he's about to say something, but he sips his coffee again instead.

Skylar turns to me. "Show him the pictures and videos, Abbi."

I hand my phone to Mr. Boyce. Luckily I'd put all the tree house pictures into a special folder; he wouldn't see the ones of Skylar and me wearing Ms. Freeman's sexy clothes. We'd experimented with her makeup and posed in crazy positions, laughing ourselves silly. If Mr. Boyce saw them, I'd die.

"I started taking these the first day we saw the cars." I watch him scroll slowly through the pictures. "This is the day they had the fight. We could hear their voices, but not what they were saying. Here's Ms. Sullivan walking across the field by herself. You can tell she's mad by the way she walks. And look, the man drives away so fast he skids on the gravel."

"We think he went somewhere and then came back and found her in the woods," Skylar says. "That's when he killed her."

Mr. Boyce scrolls through the photos and videos, then goes back to the beginning and scrolls again, pausing every now and then to study one. He's upset, I can tell by his face and the way he stares at the pictures. Maybe it's a mistake to show them to him when he's so sad about Ms. Sullivan.

Finally Mr. Boyce puts the phone down and looks at Skylar and me. "I don't understand why you took these pictures." He makes it sound like we did something wrong. "What were you thinking?" he asks. "Why were you so interested in these people?"

Skylar discovers that her stool rotates, and she turns this way and that while she tries to explain. It's the kind of thing she does when she's nervous.

"We thought they might be criminals," she tells

him, "or spies like on that TV show about these supposedly ordinary Americans who are really Russian spies. It was a mystery. We wanted to solve it."

Mr. Boyce sips his coffee slowly, his forehead wrinkled, as if he's thinking. Finally he puts the empty cup down.

"What kind of advice do you want from me?" He sounds disappointed in us. Maybe we're not so super-duper after all.

Skylar stops spinning and leans toward him. "Should we tell the police what we saw? Should we show them the stuff on the phone?"

Mr. Boyce gets up to brew another coffee. While he's waiting for the machine to beep, he walks to the sliding door that overlooks the backyard. The glass is smeared with Andy's fingerprints. The deck needs staining or painting or something, and the uncut lawn is weedier than the front yard. Big plastic toys are scattered around, some of them broken. A rusty barbecue tilts to one side. The ashes from the last time it was used are still in the grate.

For a few minutes he stands with his back to us, looking at the yard. He must miss Andy. Maybe that's why weeds have taken over and the house is so dirty.

"What should we do?" Skylar asks in a louder voice. Maybe he didn't hear her the first time.

He turns around slowly. "Abbi, if you can get along

without your phone until tomorrow, I'll look at the pictures again. I want to examine them, think about what they mean, and then make a decision about the police. Does that sound like a good idea?"

Skylar notices me hesitating. "Let Mr. Boyce have it," she says. "We came here for his advice."

"But my *phone*," I say. How will I get along without it? I use it all the time. It's like an extra organ that helps me function.

Mr. Boyce rests his hand on my shoulder. Up close he smells like he needs a shower, and his breath is straight coffee fumes. "You know what I say in class," he says. "You kids are addicted to your electronic devices. Consider this a first step toward breaking the addiction." He smiles sort of half-heartedly. "Cold turkey."

"But—"

"You can do it, Abbi!" Mr. Boyce smiles at us. "The super-duper dynamic duo, my all-time favorite students, brilliant and beautiful."

We grin at each other. We want to dance and sing and be brilliant and beautiful forever.

"So I can keep it till tomorrow?" Mr. Boyce asks me.

"Sure." I smile at him. "Cold turkey."

"Good girl." He pockets my phone. "Now, if you'll forgive me, I have errands to run."

We take the hint and ride away on our bikes. As we

coast down the hill on Third Street, we both raise our hands over our heads and shout, "Brilliant and beautiful! Super-duper dynamic duo!"

At home, we collapse on my back porch and guzzle sodas. *Brilliant and beautiful,* I think, *brilliant and beautiful.* But I don't feel brilliant and beautiful now. In fact I feel dumb and ugly. I shouldn't have given my phone to Mr. Boyce. It's like I handed him my life. But how can you say no to your favorite teacher, especially when you're one half of the super-duper dynamic duo?

I glance at Skylar. She's scrolling through her phone, reading messages. Thanks to my stupidity, I can't look at *my* messages. But Mr. Boyce can. He can look at all my photos, even the secret ones of Skylar and me dressed up in her mom's clothes. I feel my face get red just thinking about it.

Skylar looks up. "Are you mad because I have my phone and you don't?"

"No. I'm mad at myself for giving mine to Mr. Boyce."

"He needs it to make a decision about the police. You'll survive until tomorrow."

"I guess so." I hesitate to say what's on my mind, but finally I blurt it out. "Did Mr. Boyce seem a little . . . I don't know, not like himself?"

"Of course he's not his usual self," Skylar says. "For

one thing, he's really upset about Ms. Sullivan, plus he's all alone. He must miss Andy a lot."

It seems to me there's more to it. The way he looked, the coffee he kept drinking, the mess in the house.

I glance at Skylar, but she's bent over her phone, thumbs flying. Maybe she's right. Mr. Boyce is sad, that's all. I'm overreacting the way I always do, imagining things I can't even put into words.

I watch a butterfly land on a big zinnia in Mom's garden and fan its wings. A monarch, I think. It looks so fragile, yet it will fly all the way to Mexico, and in the spring, it will fly all the way back here. How is that even possible?

I reach for my phone to take its picture—and remember Mr. Boyce has it.

9

That night, I have terrible dreams. In the worst one, Ms. Sullivan lies in the woods, almost hidden under branches and plastic bags. She's wearing her sundress, I can see the little flowers. Suddenly her head is the deer's head and she's looking at me with one eye. Flies buzz, crows shriek, snakes twist down tree trunks and slither toward me. I try to run, but I can't. I try to scream, but I can't. Paul comes out of the dark, snakes coiling around his arms. "Like what you see?" he asks.

I wake up and crawl into bed with Mom. I haven't done that since first grade. Or was it third grade?

In the morning, Mom smooths my hair out of my face. "Bad dreams?"

"Ms. Sullivan," I say, "and the dead deer."

"Dead deer? Where did that come from?"

I almost say I saw it in the woods, but just in time

I remember that Mom doesn't know about the deer or the woods. "I don't know," I say. "It was just there."

Mom doesn't turn on the TV this morning. I manage to get through breakfast without crying. Neither one of us talks about Ms. Sullivan.

As she gets ready to leave for work, she asks, "Will you be all right today?"

"I think so."

She gives me a hug and a kiss. "Call me if you need me, even if it's just to talk. Stay safe. Don't let Skylar talk you into leaving the neighborhood. The police still haven't arrested anyone."

"Don't worry so much," I tell her. "I'll be fine."

A few minutes after Mom leaves, Skylar comes over. Before she even has a chance to sit down, the landline rings. I check the caller ID and see Mr. Boyce's name.

"It's him."

I try to hand the phone to Skylar but she shakes her head. "I talked to him yesterday."

"I know, but—" I look at her. "You're better at it than I am."

She backs away. "Your turn. He called your house, not mine."

The phone continues to ring. One more and it will go to message. I lift the receiver and press talk. "Hello?"

"Abbi, this is Mr. Boyce. I need to talk to you and Skylar about your pictures."

He sounds nervous, as if there's something he isn't saying.

"What do you think of them?" I ask. "Should we show them to the police?"

He hesitates, clears his throat. "Why don't you come over here? I'd really like to talk to you in person about the pictures."

"Right now?"

"Great, that's great. See you soon." He hangs up before I even have a chance to say goodbye.

"What's that all about?" Skylar asks. "He sounded kind of mad."

"Not mad," I say. "More like he's worried. Like we're in danger or something."

"Maybe he saw something in the pictures that we didn't."

"Like what?"

"How do I know?"

She's on the edge of a bad mood, so I don't ask her anything else.

We get on our bikes and begin the long ride to Mr. Boyce's house. Thanks to Skylar, I expect the killer to be driving every black SUV I see. None of the SUVs slow down when they pass us. Even so, by the time we get to Mr. Boyce's street I'm a total nervous wreck.

Today's local paper lies on the porch steps. Ms. Sullivan's face is on the front page.

Skylar folds it to hide Ms. Sullivan and hands it to Mr. Boyce when he opens the door. He tosses it on a chair already loaded with unopened mail and newspapers. He looks tired, but at least his hair's combed and he's shaved and his shirt is clean.

But he seems more upset than yesterday, kind of worried and agitated. His eyes have dark shadows under them, like he hasn't slept well.

He hands me my phone, and it's like he's given me the Holy Grail. I put it carefully into my backpack. My body has gotten back its missing part.

We follow Mr. Boyce into the kitchen. "About your pictures." He runs his hand through his hair. "Frankly, I hate to disappoint you, but I don't think they'll be very helpful. Most of them are pretty blurry, and it's hard to see important details."

I stare at him, mortified. It's like I failed a photography test.

"The police have ways to enlarge photos and enhance them," Skylar says. "They can make them almost perfect."

"In crime shows, maybe," Mr. Boyce says, "but in real life, the police can't do half the things they do on TV."

"But," I say, "shouldn't we tell them what we saw?"

"The police are most certainly aware of the SUV.

You've watched enough crime shows to know that some details of a crime aren't disclosed to the public."

He pauses. "Don't forget. You're very young and you have no evidence. The police might suspect you're making it all up just to get your names and faces on the news."

From the way he looks at Skylar and me, it seems as if Mr. Boyce might think the same thing himself. After a whole year in his class, he must know us better than that. Tears prick my eyes and I turn my head to hide them. I don't want his tissues. I don't want anything from him.

Reaching for his coffee cup, he adds, "My advice is to forget about solving crimes à la Nancy Drew and focus on important things—like your summer reading list." He tries for a big, friendly grin, but his eyes aren't smiling.

"You sound like a teacher," Skylar says.

Mr. Boyce laughs, but Skylar isn't trying to be funny. Like me, she's annoyed by his mention of Nancy Drew. I thought he took kids seriously, but here he is talking down to us the way most adults do.

While I'm fuming to myself, Mr. Boyce refills his cup. He doesn't offer Skylar and me a cold drink even though it's hotter today than it was yesterday and the two of us are just as sweaty. He stands there drinking his coffee and looking like he wishes we'd leave.

Just as I'm about to grab Skylar and head out the door, I notice an art book on a small table near me. It's the very same one I'd seen in the gray car.

I hold it up so Mr. Boyce can see it. "I saw this book in Ms. Sullivan's car."

Mr. Boyce takes it. "Kris and I used to talk about art in the faculty lounge. She recommended it, so I bought my own copy."

He opens the book and turns the pages slowly. His face is sadder than sad, and I feel like hugging him and saying I'm sad, too. We all are.

But we can't hug teachers, and they can't hug us, especially men teachers.

In fact, now that I think about it, Skylar and I shouldn't even be in Mr. Boyce's house. He'd be in trouble if anyone found out.

Skylar nudges me. "We ought to go."

Mr. Boyce looks up from the pages. "Please don't bother the police with those pictures. They've already got enough on their hands without a couple of would-be girl detectives bothering them."

I'm insulted all over again. Without even saying goodbye, I follow Skylar outside. She looks down the driveway. At the end is Mr. Boyce's Mini Cooper, the car he drives to school every day. We see him sometimes while we're waiting for the bus. He always smiles and gives us a thumbs-up for the day ahead of us.

He didn't smile today, not even once. Or yesterday either. He treated us as if we were idiot "girl detectives." He wasn't the Mr. Boyce who talks about poetry and thinks all his students are amazing, especially Skylar and me. He's a stranger who smells like beer and coffee.

Skylar says, "It's not here."

"What's not here?"

"The SUV."

"What are you talking about? Mr. Boyce has a Mini Cooper. It's right there at the end of the driveway."

"He also has a black SUV with a humongous car seat in the back for Andy. I've seen him at Food Lion with his wife and Andy, loading groceries into it."

"You never told me that."

"I didn't think it was important then, but now—with the way he's acting—"

"No." I shake my head hard. "All SUVs look the same. There must be hundreds of them in Evansburg. I see them everywhere."

"Listen to me, Abbi." Skylar grips her handlebars. She's straddling her bike, ready to ride, but not until she's told me what she's thinking. Even if I don't want to hear it.

"They both taught at the same school," she says. "He has the art book we saw in her car. And you saw him at the pool with his wife . . . you saw how angry she was. Mr. Boyce is the mystery man, Abbi. He was having an affair with Ms. Sullivan—which makes him a suspect big-time."

I keep shaking my head, but not as hard as before. "If he has an SUV, why isn't it in the driveway?"

"Because his wife drove it to her mother's house. It's got Andy's car seat."

Skylar is clicking puzzle pieces together way too fast. "Ms. Sullivan would never have an affair with a married man," I say, "and neither would he, not with Andy and all—"

"He's a cheater, like my dad. *He* had kids, my mom really loved him, but that didn't stop him from leaving us and ruining our lives." She pauses and glares at me. "And Ms. Sullivan was a cheater, too. She knew he was married, she knew he had a kid, but all she cared about was breaking up his marriage so he could be with her. In some ways, she's worse than he is."

I don't want to believe any of this. It's all a tangle in my head, and I can't make sense of it. I love Mr. Boyce, I love Ms. Sullivan. It was wrong of them to have an affair, but they're not bad people. They fell in love with each other, they couldn't help it. Blame Venus, the goddess with no arms.

But there's no way to argue with Skylar, not when she's all worked up about her dad.

She pushes off and starts pedaling. I ride after her. "Where are you going?"

"The police station. Where else?"

My mouth doesn't want to say the words, but I push them out anyway. "Do you think Mr. Boyce killed Ms. Sullivan?"

Her eyes narrow to slits. She is merciless. "He could have."

"I'll never believe that," I tell her. "Not Mr. Boyce. He might have an affair, but he'd never kill anybody."

"You watch the same cop shows I watch," Skylar says. "The major suspect is always the husband or the boyfriend. No matter how nice they seem, the police go after them first."

My legs feel too weak to push the pedals. She's right about crime shows. What if she's right about Mr. Boyce, too?

The police station is only a few blocks away. We both ride slowly, slowly, slowly, barely pedaling, but we get there anyway.

We lock our bikes to a rack and stand at the bottom of the steps, looking up at the big glass door. We've never been inside a police station.

We climb the steps one at a time, like kids with little short legs. On Main Street people go in and out of stores. Cars and bikes go by. It's just an ordinary day for everybody but Skylar and me.

The glass door doesn't open automatically. We push hard. It's very heavy.

Inside, I expect to see criminals shouting and cursing and carrying on, but the room is more like the post office—except there aren't any lines.

A policeman smiles at us from behind a plexiglass barrier. "What can I do for you girls today? Lost dog or cat maybe? Stolen bike?"

We approach him cautiously. "It's a lot more serious than that." Skylar's voice comes out high-pitched like that of a scared child.

I move behind her, hoping she'll do all the talking.

The policeman's smile fades a bit as he waits for her to go on.

Skylar gulps and takes a deep breath. "We have something to tell you about Ms. Sullivan." Her voice is a whisper now, and she has to repeat herself before the policeman understands.

"Hold it right there. I'll get Detective Klein." He goes through a doorway. We hear him say something. A tall, thin man appears. He looks like a TV detective, the kind who takes one look at a person and knows everything worth knowing.

"I'm Detective Klein," he says. "And you are?"

We tell him our names. I have to say mine twice because I'm too scared to speak up. He takes us to his office and gives us sodas.

We open the cans and take a few sips. I choke on mine, and some goes up my nose and makes me cough.

Except for the way one of her legs jiggles, Skylar looks totally calm.

Detective Klein waits patiently. "What is it you want to tell me about Ms. Sullivan?"

All of a sudden I realize how serious this is. Skylar and I are here to tell a detective what we saw. He might arrest Mr. Boyce. He might put him in jail. This is real life, not a detective show.

I want to go home, but I've already drunk half the soda Detective Klein gave me. It's like I've accepted a bribe. I can't leave now.

Skylar says, "Ms. Sullivan was Abbi's art teacher. She used to meet Mr. Boyce, our language arts teacher, every Thursday at the end of Marie Drive. She'd get in his car and they'd drive away together."

Detective Klein raises his eyebrows. "How do you know this?"

"We saw them from our tree house," Skylar says. "We didn't know who they were then. He never got out of the SUV and she wore huge sunglasses and a big straw hat that hid her face and hair."

Skylar pauses to drink her soda, and I finally find my voice. "One day they had a big argument. Ms. Sullivan got out of Mr. Boyce's SUV and ran across the field into the woods. We thought he'd go after her, but he drove away fast, like he was really mad."

Skylar finishes her soda. "He could have come back

and met up with her in the woods. Maybe they had another argument, and he—"

She hesitates and glances at me. I swallow hard and hope she won't finish the sentence.

"Well, we kind of think he might have killed her," she whispers.

"But we're not sure," I say. "We didn't actually see him come back to look for her."

Detective Klein waits a minute, as if he thinks we might have more to say. When we just sit there, he asks, "How do you know the car belonged to Ms. Sullivan?"

"We didn't at first," Skylar says. "After she went missing, we saw the car on the news. It was gray like the one we saw, and the license plate was the same: 3MB5098."

He leans forward and stares at us. It's like he knows everything about us, even that we used to steal candy from Madison Market on our way home from grade school. "Is the car still on Marie Drive?"

"I don't know. Maybe. We haven't gone there for a while," Skylar says.

"The last time we saw it," I say, "a window was broken and her purse and phone were gone."

"Why didn't you report this?" he asks. "You saw the news. You knew it was important evidence."

"We were scared," Skylar says, "especially after we heard that Ms. Sullivan was murdered. We wanted to get somebody's advice, so we went to see Mr. Boyce."

"Wait." Detective Klein stares at Skylar. "You told Mr. Boyce what you saw, even though you thought he might have killed Ms. Sullivan?"

Skylar's face droops like she might cry. "He was our favorite teacher. We loved him. Everybody does. We didn't know then that he was the man in the SUV."

"I'm confused. Help me out here." Detective Klein gives us that piercing look again. "What makes you think Mr. Boyce killed Ms. Sullivan?"

"He has an SUV just like the one we saw on Marie Drive. He had the art book we saw in her car. And—" Skylar pauses a second. "He told us not to show you the pictures and not to bother you with a lot of kid detective stuff."

"What pictures?"

"The ones on my phone. They're not very good, but you can see the license plates on both cars."

Detective Klein holds out his hand. "Give me the phone, please."

I scroll to the folder of pictures and hand him the phone.

He clicks on the icon and looks at me. "You must have given me the wrong folder. This one is empty."

I take the phone. He's right. The pictures and videos are gone.

Skylar leans over and stares at the screen. "He must have deleted them," she whispers.

"No," I say. "My phone saves them for a few weeks before they get permanently deleted. You know, in case you change your mind." While I talk, I'm clicking on the menu, looking for the trash icon. I open it. All I see is text: *No Images. Your library is empty.*

"He's erased *everything*," Skylar says. "Every single picture you ever took is gone."

Detective Klein says, "Don't worry. We can get them back. They're still in the Cloud."

"My iCloud storage is full and Mom can't afford more." I start crying again.

Detective Klein shoves a box of tissues toward me and I take one. "I'll keep the phone for a while," he says. "Maybe there's a way to get the pictures back."

He puts my phone into a plastic bag. I write my name and address on a label. I watch him stick it on the bag. I blow my nose and stop crying. I'm scared to ask how long the police will keep my phone.

Detective Klein straightens a pile of papers on his desk. "Do you by any chance remember the license plate number of the SUV? Or the make and model?"

Skylar is a genius at remembering numbers.

"Maryland 9PS4227. It was a Ford, but I don't know the model or the year."

"Thank you," he says. "That should be helpful."

He leans back in his chair and studies us with his X-ray eyes. I'm hoping this is all, and we can go now.

Skylar is actually halfway to her feet when he says, "I want you both to make a statement about what you saw, but because you're minors, your parents must be present. I'll come to your homes this evening."

Neither of us had expected this. "No, please," I beg. "My mom will kill me."

"We'll be grounded for the rest of our lives," Skylar says.

Detective Klein smiles. "That might not be a bad idea."

He stands up and shakes our hands. "Thanks for coming in, girls. Even though I wish we'd known this sooner, what you've told us might be helpful."

At the door, Detective Klein says, "For your own safety, leave solving crimes to us. Don't get involved in things you don't understand. Nancy Drew isn't anything like real life."

Skylar and I wince. We detest Nancy Drew now.

He holds the door open. We walk out feeling worse than we did before we came.

10

We haven't ridden far when I hear someone yelling our names. I look over my shoulder and see Jason and Carter riding toward us on their fancy bikes, bent over their handlebars, pedaling hard to catch up.

We pedal harder, but a hill slows us down.

Jason pulls in front of us and Carter skids to a stop beside me. "What were you doing at the police station?" Carter asks.

Skylar tries to stare him down. "Who says we were at the police station?"

Carter sneers at her. "We saw your bikes in the rack." He moves his bike so close to hers, the handlebars touch. "You better not have told them about that Honda. Or us, or anything else you think you know."

"Maybe we were selling Girl Scout cookies," Skylar says. "Cops like to snack while they drink their coffee." She's trying to flip him off, show him he can't tell her what to do, but I know Skylar well enough to tell she's getting scared. I'm already scared. There's something different about the boys today. They're jittery, like there's something bad going on.

Carter nudges her bike with his foot. Skylar almost loses her balance but keeps the bike upright. "Back off," she tells him. "Your breath stinks."

Carter looks like he might hit her, and I grab her arm. "Come on, Skylar, let's go."

She shakes me off. "He can't tell me what to do."

All this time Jason's been sitting on his bike saying nothing, just watching. Now he coasts closer. "Get out of here, both of you," he says. "You got no idea what's going on."

Skylar glares at him. "Oh, like *you* know so much."

Jason dumps his bike and grabs Skylar's handlebars. His face is close to hers. She draws back like he's a snake about to bite. "We know stuff that would blow your mind," he says.

Carter shoves him away from Skylar. "Shut up, Jason."

Jason turns on Carter. "You're not the boss of me." To Skylar he says, "You think you're so smart. Even the cops don't know what we know."

Carter grabs the neck of Jason's T-shirt and twists it until Jason chokes. "Shut up! Are you nuts or what?"

I start to ride away, but Skylar's still standing there,

watching them fight. Jason punches Carter, and Carter punches him back. They grab each other like wrestlers and grunt and strain and struggle until Jason's face turns so red I think he's dying of heatstroke. Cars go by without even slowing down. It's like no one cares what's going on here.

"Quit it!" I shout at them. "Quit it!"

The boys break apart. Their chests heave, they pant, their T-shirts are soaked with sweat. Jason's nose is bleeding and Carter's lip is cut. It scares me to see how much damage they've done to each other.

Without saying anything else to us, they jump on their bikes and coast downhill, heading back the way they came, toward Marie Drive. "Just keep your stupid mouths shut," Carter yells over his shoulder. "No more cops!"

Skylar watches them through slitted eyes. "We should've let them kill each other," she mutters to me. Turning her bike around, she prepares to push off.

"Where are you going?" I ask.

"Come on," she says. "We're following them."

"You're crazy," I say.

"I bet they know where the phone and purse are," Skylar says. "If we follow them, we can tell Detective Klein. He'll take us seriously then. Maybe we'll even get a reward."

This is a bad idea, one of the worst Skylar's ever had.

I stand there and watch her ride away. "Come back," I yell after her. "Come back!"

Skylar keeps going, picking up speed as she races downhill. Once she gets an idea into her head, you can't stop her. I'll tell her what I think when I catch up with her. For now, there's nothing to do but push off and ride after her. She's my best friend. No matter how stupid she is, I can't let her ride off alone. What if something happened to her? What if she never came back?

On Marie Drive, the little houses sit silently on their neatly mowed lawns, but no one is in sight. Somebody cuts the grass, somebody waters the flowers, somebody brings in the mail, but we never see them. They either work or stay inside all day. It's like a science fiction movie where everyone has died of the plague or been killed by aliens from outer space.

We stop near the end of the road and listen. Up ahead, out of sight, I hear Carter swearing at Jason. Yelling words I'd never say. Jason swears back at him. All they do is swear and swear without saying anything that makes sense.

Skylar creeps closer as if she thinks she might hear something important, but the boys move on across the field, still swearing and shoving each other.

Ms. Sullivan's car is gone. Either the police towed it away or somebody stole it.

We lay our bikes in the weeds by the side of the road and watch the boys until they reach the edge of the woods. From here, they're about the size of my thumb—too little to be dangerous.

After the woods swallow them up, Skylar and I sprint across the field. I stop, scared to go farther, but Skylar beckons me to follow her into the trees. I hesitate. The sunlight warms my back, but the woods ahead are full of shadows. Somewhere out of sight I hear crows calling, as if they're warning me. The dead deer flashes across my mind. I can almost smell it. I shouldn't be here. I should be home, safe from the danger I sense all around me.

Ms. Sullivan died here. Maybe it wasn't Mr. Boyce who killed her. Maybe it was someone or something else. Something that lives in these woods, something evil.

Skylar beckons again. She's angry now. I shake my head, afraid to follow her. She shrugs, turns her back, and walks away.

I'm not like Mr. Boyce. I hurry after Skylar, taking care to make as little noise as possible. *Whatever happens, happens,* I tell myself.

When I catch up with her, she says, "Go home if you're so scared. I don't need you."

"Yes, you do," I say. "And I need you."

She squeezes my hand, and we sneak through the trees. We freeze for a second when we hear the boys. They're closer than we thought.

Keeping a safe distance, we follow them. We're a lot quieter than they are. After about fifteen minutes they stop and shush each other. We squat in the underbrush and wait to see what they do next.

They're standing behind a tree, staring at a trailer. It's streaked green with moss and almost invisible; its windows are covered with cardboard. Though it looks deserted, I see a big, shiny padlock on the door.

I don't need my imagination to tell me this is a dangerous place. I whisper in Skylar's ear, "Let's go before someone sees us." I start backing away as quietly as I can, but Skylar shakes her head.

"We can't leave now," she whispers. "This is just like a crime show. We might even get on the local news. *Brave girls solve murder.* . . . How does that sound?"

I don't answer. All I want to do is get out of these woods alive.

Carter and Jason run behind the trailer in a half crouch, like soldiers in a war movie.

The thing is, this is not a crime show and it's not a war movie. Am I the only one who knows that?

Moving from tree to tree, we find a good watching place. Jason and Carter grab the edges of a camouflage tarpaulin and struggle to pull it off whatever's hidden underneath. They almost fall over backwards, but they finally succeed. It's Ms. Sullivan's car—or what's left of it. The tires are gone, the doors are gone, the seats are gone. Even the dashboard, the console, and the glove compartment are gone. We wouldn't have known it was hers if we hadn't seen the license plate lying in the weeds.

Skylar and I huddle so close together I can almost hear her heart beating. Except for the license plate, there's nothing left to prove that Ms. Sullivan owned this car. There's no sense of her as my teacher, as an artist, as a really special person I will never see again. I picture her driving to the end of Marie Drive the day she disappeared forever. She must have been angry with him. He let her down, I guess, and she left him sitting in his SUV with Andy's car seat in the back. It was all so sad.

If only she hadn't fallen in love with him, if only he'd been who we thought he was.

Carter swears and draws my attention back to him and Jason. "He's stripped it already."

"Let's go," Jason says. "There's nothing left to take."

As they walk away, we hear an engine.

Jason looks over his shoulder. "Someone's coming!" The boys run toward us and dive into the bushes a heartbeat away from Skylar and me. We freeze.

Paul's red pickup comes up a dirt driveway and stops near the trailer. He shuts off the engine and sits and listens before he gets out. A big black dog jumps from the back of the truck. If it smells us, we're dead. Nobody moves. Nobody even breathes.

The dog stops to pee and then follows Paul. I'm too scared to watch them, so I close my eyes like a kid at a horror movie. I knew something like this would happen.

I hear the key turn in the padlock and then the squeak of the door. After it closes softly, I open my eyes. The trailer looks as deserted as before, but I know Paul and his dog are in there.

That's when Carter and Jason notice us. They stare at us like they're in shock.

"What are you doing here?" Carter growls.

"We followed you," Skylar says.

Carter punches Jason so hard he topples over. "I told you not to say anything, and what do you do? Blab to this dog who can't keep her nose out of anything."

Jason moans and sort of rocks back and forth. "Shut up, shut up, shut up. If Diablo hears us, we're dead."

I huddle deeper into myself, too terrified to say anything. I feel a flash of dislike for Skylar. If it wasn't for her, I'd be safe at home.

11

We sit in the bushes, scared to move, scared to talk. Bugs crawl on us. Mosquitoes bite us. It's hot, humid. No breeze. Nothing seems real. Not the woods, not the trailer, not the dog, not Paul. This can't be happening to Skylar and me.

Skylar tosses an acorn at Carter to get his attention. "Are we going to sit here all afternoon or what?" she whispers. "It must be after four. My mother expects me home for dinner."

Carter stares at her with mean eyes. "What planet do you live on?"

Skylar gives him a look just as mean as the one he gave her. "Earth, last time I checked."

"There's a man and a dog in that trailer," Carter says. "If Diablo hears you and starts barking, Paul's going to let him out. He's a killer, that dog. He'll tear you apart."

"The dog's not the only killer," Jason whispers. He's gone ashy white with fear.

Carter cuffs him. "Shut up. You want him to hear you?"

Jason clenches his fists. "*You* shut up."

When they start swearing again, Skylar nudges me. We start crawling away, but Carter grabs my foot and yanks me back.

"Nobody goes anywhere till I say so."

"Are you stupid or what?" Skylar says. "The longer we sit here, the more dangerous it is. What if somebody comes along to buy drugs? What if Paul lets Diablo out to poop?"

Jason says, "She's right. We ought to get out of here while we can."

"Don't listen to her," Carter says. "She's nothing but a dumb girl."

I realize that both Carter and Jason are even more scared than we are. Maybe because they know Paul a lot better than we do.

"Leave him here," Skylar tells Jason. "It's three against one."

Jason looks at Carter like he isn't sure who to side with. Carter slowly gets to his hands and knees. "Let's go," he says, as if it's his idea to leave.

Carefully we crawl through the underbrush, holding branches to keep them from rustling. As the trees

141

close in around us, we feel safer and move faster, half bent over, keeping low.

Behind us, we hear the trailer door open. Paul says, "Go on, Diablo, do your business."

We freeze in place. We see the dog, but maybe we're too far away for him to smell us. Or the wind's wrong.

Diablo goes straight to the place where we'd hidden. He sniffs, then raises his head and barks. In a second, the dog's on our trail. Somewhere behind him, Paul shouts at us to stop. "I'm warning you. I got a gun!"

Paul shoots into the woods. The crows go crazy. A bullet thuds into a tree close enough to scare me so much I almost wet my pants. He can't see us—the woods hide us—but he shoots again and again.

The boys scatter, but Skylar and I stay together. We have no idea which way to go. Or where Marie Drive is. We just flat-out run, dodging trees and ducking under vines, plowing through weeds and brambles, splashing through puddles and jumping over fallen branches. We can still hear the gun but it's farther away now. He must be shooting at the boys, not us.

If we live through this, I will never leave my neighborhood again, not even my yard.

We come to the Paint Branch and plunge down the bank and into the water. It's hip-deep, the stones on the bottom slippery, but we keep going. We've both read enough books to know that Diablo can't track us if we stay in the water. I hope it's true.

By the time we reach the railroad bridge, we've slipped and fallen so often we're totally soaked. Even our hair is wet. We know where we are, but we're scared to come out of the water. If Diablo finds us, he can run across the bridge and get us. So we sit on the bank under the bridge and listen. All we hear are crows and the noise of cars bumping over the tracks in town. Evansburg is so close, yet so far away. At least we don't hear the gun anymore.

Skylar gets out her phone, but her hands are wet and she drops it. We watch in shock as it sinks in the muddy water. Even if we find it, it won't work now.

I hear a splashing sound up around a bend in the stream. Someone is wading toward us, but I can't see who it is. Skylar and I crawl farther under the bridge, but there's really nowhere to hide. We huddle together and watch the stream to see who's coming—Diablo or Paul?

Jason splashes into sight, breathing hard. For the first time in my life, I'm glad to see him. I still hate him, but he's a lot better than Paul or Diablo.

Without saying a word, he slumps against the red clay bank, half in the water, half out. His wet T-shirt clings to his belly, his face is streaked with snot and tears and mud, and his hair sticks up in clumps.

"Where's Carter?" Skylar asks.

"Back there somewhere." He's still breathing hard. "We split, and Diablo went after him."

"Was Paul shooting at us?" I ask.

"He's crazy." Jason wipes snot off his face with his T-shirt. "He probably thought we were trying to steal his meth."

We sit under the bridge. Nobody says anything. Not even Skylar. I try not to think about Diablo attacking Carter. Or Paul shooting him. I hate Carter, but I don't want anything bad to happen to him. I don't want anything to happen to Jason either. I especially don't want anything to happen to Skylar and me.

"Didn't me and Carter tell you to stop messing with us?" Jason asks. "Didn't we say you don't have any business coming here and spying on us?"

"We weren't spying on you," Skylar says. "All we wanted was a nice quiet place to read, and then you and Carter came along and ruined everything. This is all your fault."

"Don't blame me and Carter," Jason says. "If you'd stayed home and minded your own business, you wouldn't be sitting under this bridge."

"If you hadn't been selling drugs," Skylar says, "you wouldn't be sitting here either."

"That's why you went to the police station, isn't it?" Jason asks. "You told them me and Carter were selling weed."

This is still the same day we went to the police station? It seems way longer ago than that—a week at least, maybe even a lifetime.

"Oh, sure, it's all about you," Skylar says. "Well, here's some news for you. Abbi and I were spying on the cars that used to park under the tree house, not on you. We went to the police to tell them that Mr. Boyce killed Ms. Sullivan."

"Mr. Boyce—the teacher at our school? *That* Mr. Boyce?" Jason has a weird look on his face, like he can't believe what he's just heard. "You really think a guy like him could kill somebody?"

"He was having an affair with her." Skylar is as sure of herself as ever. "They had a fight. She got mad and walked off. Abbi and I saw her go into the woods. Later he found her and killed her." She folds her arms across her chest. "Case closed."

"You are so wrong," Jason says. "Boyce didn't kill her."

"Well, if he didn't, who did?" Skylar isn't about to back down. She's made up her mind. A moron like Jason isn't going to change anything.

Normally, I wouldn't believe a word that comes out

of Jason's mouth. But he's not his usual self. He's scared. The puzzle pieces are changing, they're forming a new picture.

"Okay, this is what happened," Jason says in a low, flat voice, like a little kid telling us about a movie he saw. "Carter and me were smoking in the woods behind the trailer, waiting for Paul to come back and give us some pot to sell. We saw Ms. Sullivan. I don't know what she was doing in the woods—she must have got lost or something—and I was about to say something to her, but Paul drove up and saw her behind the trailer. He must've been out of his mind on drugs. I don't even know what he took, just something bad. He accused her of being after his drug money. He was swearing and shouting and then he hit her. And he hit her, and he hit her again, and he just kept hitting her. And she was yelling, fighting back, but, but—" Jason covers his face with his hands and starts crying, awful gulping sounds that come from his gut like nothing I ever heard before.

Skylar and I put our arms around each other tight, tight, and start crying too. I want the words Jason just said to go back into his mouth like a movie running backwards. I can't stand knowing that Paul hurt Ms. Sullivan.

"I hate him. He's a freaking crazy man. A psycho."

Jason snuffles snot back up his nose. He rubs his eyes with his fists like a child. "I swear there's nothing Carter and me could've done to stop him. It was like he didn't know what he was doing, like he couldn't stop."

While Jason is telling us this, I look at Skylar. Her head is down, her hair hiding her face. She's still crying and so am I. She must be thinking what I'm thinking. Mr. Boyce didn't do it. We were wrong. We made a terrible mistake.

Jason wipes his nose on the sleeve of his shirt. For a while no one says anything. The crows are silent. No gunshots. No barking dog. Just the cars going over the railroad tracks in town.

"I wish I never seen it," Jason mutters. "I wish I never was there, never had nothing to do with Paul."

Skylar looks at him with disgust. "How did you meet a lowlife like him anyway?"

"He's Carter's uncle," Jason says. "Carter never told me nothing about him except he was a dealer and he wanted us to sell drugs at the high school. It sounded like a good deal." He sighs and looks at me. "Remember that night at the DQ when your mom's boyfriend kept Paul from beating me up?"

I think of Paul's muscles and tattoos and how he looked ready to pound Jason to a pulp and what Greg said about him. I think of how he scared Skylar and me at the gas station. I almost feel sorry for Jason.

"That's when I should've figured out what kind of guy Paul is."

Skylar gives him her worst deadeye look. "But you stuck with him because you wanted to sell pot to kids like my brother."

Jason looks down like he's ashamed. "We needed cash," he mutters.

Skylar scrambles to her feet. "I'm done talking to you," she tells Jason. "Come on, Abbi, we're going home."

I turn to Jason. "Is it safe? Is he still looking for us? Will he kill us?"

"Maybe he won't find out you were with Carter and me. *I* won't tell him."

"What about Carter?" I ask. "Will *he*?"

Jason lowers his head. "I don't know," he mutters. "Go home, go on. Get out of here."

"But what about you?" I ask. "Where are you going?"

Jason looks surprised that I care where he's going. "I can't go home. Paul knows where I live. Maybe I could stay with my dad for a while. His girlfriend hates me, but, well—" He shrugs and looks at us as if he thinks we can help him somehow. He's so pitiful I can hardly stand it.

Skylar tugs on my arm. "Let's go. Jason can take care of himself."

As we start to walk away, Jason runs after us. "Wait! Don't leave me here. If he finds me, he'll kill me."

Skylar keeps walking, but I look back. Jason's limping. Blood runs down his leg and leaves drops in the dirt behind him. I yank Skylar's arm to stop her. "He's hurt. He's bleeding. We can't just leave him here."

Skylar pulls away from me. "What do you want to do? Take him home with you?"

By now Jason has caught up with us. He's breathing too hard to say anything.

"Did Diablo bite you?" Skylar asks.

"I fell on something, I don't know what. It was sharp and it hurt." He looks over his shoulder as if he expects to see Paul aiming a gun at us. "We got to get out of here."

Skylar is obviously mad that Jason is with us, but she doesn't say anything. What's there to say? We're all scared of Paul. We might as well stick together. Mom has always told me there's safety in numbers. I'm not sure what that means, but still . . .

As we get closer to town, we start watching for the red pickup. We look over our shoulders, we keep close to buildings, we pause at each intersection. Nobody notices our muddy clothes or Jason's bloody leg. If you think about it, most people don't look closely at other people unless they know them. Luckily for us, everyone we pass is a stranger.

When we get to our street, Skylar says, "What do we do with him? He's not coming to my house, not after he sold drugs to my brother."

"I'll hide in your garage or something," Jason says. "Nobody will even know I'm there."

"You're so not hiding in my garage or anywhere else in my yard." She glares at him. "Drug dealer."

Jason turns to me. "How about you, Abbi? Can I stay in your garage?"

"My mom isn't home from work yet. She'll see you when she parks her car." He looks so pitiful, with his head hanging down and his shoulders hunched and his wet T-shirt still sticking to him so tightly I can see his belly button. How will I feel if he walks off by himself and Paul kills him?

I glance at Skylar. I can tell she's thinking the same thing. But she's waiting for me to solve the problem.

"There's an old shed in our backyard," I say. "Mom keeps the lawn mower and garden stuff in it. You can hide there."

We walk down our street. Skylar turns off at her house. She doesn't say goodbye to either of us.

Jason watches her run up the front steps and disappear into her house. I can tell he's thinking he'll never see her again. Which will be fine with Skylar.

I lead Jason around the side of my house and stop at the outside spigot. "Maybe you should wash the cut on your leg. I'll get some soap."

I run into the house and grab soap, a towel, and Band-Aids. Jason has rolled up one leg of his jeans and is rinsing the mud and caked blood off. He's grunting like it hurts.

The cut is deep and nasty. I think I see something white. I hope it's not his leg bone. "You need to go to the doctor and get a tetanus shot. You probably need stitches, too."

He takes the soap and starts washing the cut. "I'm okay. I don't need anything." He's trying to act tough now, like his normal self, but he can't fool me. He's still as scared as I am.

"You've been in the Paint Branch. Your cut's probably infected. Do you want to get blood poisoning?"

"It's just a cut. It won't kill me." He scrubs his leg, trying not to wince.

"Have it your way." I hand him the Band-Aids and point across the yard. "The shed's over there. You better hide. Mom will be home soon."

Mom. With everything else going on, I totally forgot that Detective Klein is coming tonight. What will she do when he rings the doorbell and tells her why he's here?

Should I warn Jason? He's halfway across the yard, limping toward the shed. If he shuts the door and stays inside, he won't see Detective Klein. And Detective Klein won't see him.

I watch the shed door close. I've got about ten minutes to get ready to face Mom.

12

I strip off my wet, muddy clothes and bury them at the bottom of my laundry basket. In the shower I run the water hot and scrub and scrub. I shampoo twice, but I still smell like the Paint Branch. Even dressed in clean clothes, I get a whiff of wet mud and pollution.

I drink three glasses of water, gulping it down so fast I nearly choke. I must have swallowed some of the Paint Branch. Maybe clean water will wash it out, or at least dilute it.

I sit on the sofa and wait for Mom. When Detective Klein gets here, she's going to find out about the tree house and all the other stuff Skylar and I have been doing. She will be furious, absolutely insane. Maybe she'll find my father and give me to him.

Her car pulls into the driveway. I want to throw myself into her arms and tell her everything, but I hold back. Right now, I need a mom who loves me, not one who's too mad at me to care if I go to jail. I'll lie my head off to keep her on my side as long as I can.

Mom comes through the door and sinks down on the couch beside me. She puts her arms around me and holds me tight. It feels so good. I'm safe now—at least until Detective Klein shows up.

"Oh, Abbi," she says, "have you heard? The police have taken Mr. Boyce in for questioning. So far, he hasn't been accused of anything, but the news team has jumped all over the story. Apparently someone on the school faculty told them he was involved with Ms. Sullivan. That makes him what the newscaster calls 'a person of interest.'"

She hugs me and kisses the top of my head. "I know how much Mr. Boyce means to you. Such a nice man, such a good teacher. It must be a terrible shock."

I cling to her and let myself cry and cry and cry. I must be really stupid, but it hadn't occurred to me that the police would actually take Mr. Boyce in for questioning. I thought they'd come to his house, ask a few questions, and leave. I never imagined that the local news would be there, sticking cameras in his face, yelling questions at him.

What if the police think he really did it? What if they put him in jail—all because of Skylar and me and our stupid detective game? I'm in tears, and Mom is trying to comfort me.

I should tell her that Detective Klein is coming. I should prepare her. I should confess, but I can't. Maybe they won't come, I tell myself, maybe after their talk with Mr. Boyce, they won't need statements from Skylar and me. He'll have an alibi, they'll see he's innocent. They won't tell him who blabbed about Ms. Sullivan and him.

"Greg wants to meet us for dinner at Gepetto's," Mom says. "Are you up for that?"

I shake my head. "I'm not hungry."

She pulls out her cell phone and texts Greg. Just as she puts her phone down, the landline rings. We're practically the only people I know who still have one, but Mom insists that we need a backup in case of a power failure.

She answers. "Yes, this is Cathy Dawson. Yes, that's correct, Abbi is my daughter."

There's a slight pause. "No, she hasn't told me. Seven o'clock. Yes, that will be fine. Thank you."

She looks at the receiver as if she wants to say more, ask some questions maybe, but I hear the dial tone. She puts the phone down gently, as if she's afraid of it.

"Abbi," she says. "What's this about? Why do the police want to talk to you? What can you tell them about Ms. Sullivan's death?"

She looks at me as if a couple of minutes on the phone have turned me into a stranger.

"Don't be mad," I beg. "Don't be mad, please don't hate me."

Her face is serious, her voice low. "No matter what it's about, Abbi, I won't hate you, but I can't guarantee I won't be mad."

Between sobs, I tell her about the tree house and what we saw and how Mr. Boyce acted at his house. I tell her about going to the police. I leave out the worst part. Even Detective Klein doesn't know what happened today.

She stares at me as if she can't speak or move. I can't tell if she's angry or shocked.

"I'm sorry." I hear the whine in my voice. I sound like I'm six years old and apologizing for crossing the street without permission.

I stumble on. "I wish I'd never gone there, Mom. It was sort of a game at first, a mystery to solve. And then when we found out who we'd been spying on, well, Skylar—"

Mom comes back to life. "Skylar," she says. "Always Skylar. You do everything she says. Don't you have a mind of your own?"

"Don't blame Skylar. It was my idea too."

Mom gets up and paces around the living room. "At

this point it doesn't really matter whose idea it was. I thought I could trust you while I was at work. It seems you still need a babysitter!"

She stops pacing and grabs my shoulders, forcing me to look into her eyes. I have a feeling she wants to shake some sense into me. Or hit me. I've never seen her this angry.

"There's no telling what could have happened to you and Skylar. You could have been hurt, you could have—you could have been—"

Mom tightens her grip on me as if that will keep me safe. "Promise me you'll never do something like this again."

"I promise, Mom. Skylar and I, we didn't—"

"Leave Skylar out of this. It's you I care about!"

She lets me go so fast I stumble backward. If she's this mad about the tree house, I hope she never finds out what else I did. I glance out the window. The shed door is closed. If Jason opens it and she sees him, it's all over.

Mom picks up her phone and calls Greg. "Change of plans," she says. "A detective is coming to take a statement from Abbi regarding Mr. Boyce and Ms. Sullivan. Can you please come over?" She lowers her voice but I hear her whisper, "I need you."

In the silence, I hear Greg buzzing away, but I can't

understand what he's saying.

"Yes," Mom says. "I'd appreciate that. We'll eat here before Detective Klein arrives."

Greg shows up with the pizza around six. I watch him open the box. Even though it's still hot and loaded with my favorite toppings, I can't eat one slice. I even hate the smell of it.

Greg looks at the uneaten pizza on my plate. "What's this about, Abs?"

"Skylar and I did something," I mumble, "and Mom—"

Mom slams some plates on the table. "You'll hear all about it when Detective Klein arrives," she tells Greg, and then goes on to give a complete recap of what I told her.

Greg stares at me. "That's the stupidest thing you've ever done. You've got no idea what goes on in that area. Druggies and dealers do their business there. You're lucky you didn't run into them."

To keep from looking at Greg and Mom, I tear my pizza into little pieces. This is the first time he's ever been mad at me.

Greg opens a beer and takes a sip. "Going to the police about your favorite teacher, though—that was pretty gutsy, Abs. Boyce didn't kill that poor woman, but I can see why you thought he did." Turning to

Mom, he adds, "Cut her some slack, Cathy. She's really upset. She won't—"

Mom looks like she's about to throw the pizza box at him. "Don't you dare take her side! Ever since Abbi was born, I've done my best to take care of her and keep her safe. You think that's easy when you're a single parent? And now look at the danger she's put herself in!"

Mom bursts into tears. Greg runs around to her side of the table and hugs her.

"Cath, Cath," he murmurs. "No one's taking sides here. Abbi knows she and Skylar shouldn't have been hanging out in that tree house spying on people. Don't be so hard on her. She's a good kid—you know that, I know that. Please, honey, you're a great mom. Kids her age do things like this."

Mom pulls away from him. She's still mad, still crying, but not as hard as before. What if she breaks up with Greg because of me?

The doorbell rings. Greg goes to answer it, and Mom tries to pull herself together. She blows her nose, wipes her eyes, and sits up straighter. She looks at me, and I look at her. *As long as she never learns about the much worse stuff I've done, it will be okay,* I think. She'll get over being mad at Greg. And at me too—but that might take longer.

When Greg comes back with Detective Klein, Mom

is rinsing plates in the sink and tidying up the kitchen. Most of the pizza is still in the box.

Detective Klein has a policewoman with him. He introduces himself and Officer Delaney. They sit down at the kitchen table with us. My empty stomach churns, and bile rises in my throat. I swallow it down and wish I was anywhere but here. After getting Mom's permission to interview me, Detective Klein puts a recorder on the table and begins.

He states his name and Officer Delaney's name. He identifies Mom and Greg and me. He states the date and place.

Then the questions begin. I answer them as truthfully as I can. I'm not as scared as I expected. It's like talking to a teacher when you forgot your homework or did badly on a test.

While I describe what we saw, I don't look at Mom, but I sense her leaning in, listening closely. I keep reminding myself that Detective Klein doesn't know about today, he doesn't know Jason is hiding in the shed, he doesn't know Paul killed Ms. Sullivan. Which means I've got to tell him. But not while Mom and Greg are sitting here. Maybe I can talk to him afterward, just him and me.

Detective Klein concludes the interview, just like they do on *Law and Order*, and turns off the recorder.

Turning to Mom, he says, "As I'm sure you know,

Abbi and Skylar put themselves in an extremely dangerous situation. Most of the drug activity here takes place in that area."

Mom tells him she plans to take my bike away and confine me to our block of Grant Street. There will be no more roaming around town looking for mysteries to solve. No more bike rides to Marie Drive. Or anywhere else.

Detective Klein nods. "I've talked to Ms. Freeman, and she has decided on a similar course of action."

He looks at me. "If I see you or Skylar outside your neighborhood, I'll pick you up and bring you home. And so will any police officer who sees you."

Turning to Mom, he asks for a picture of me to post at the station. I watch him slip it into a folder on top of a picture of Skylar. I'm totally humiliated.

The interview is over. Detective Klein hasn't asked about the woods or the trailer or Paul. He doesn't know Skylar and I were there. He doesn't know Jason is in our shed.

But Detective Klein isn't finished. He asks Mom for permission to talk to me in private.

"Officer Delaney will be with me," he says. "If you're at all uncomfortable, you can request a lawyer."

Greg frowns. "Why the secrecy?"

Detective Klein looks at me. "Abbi might not tell me certain things in front of you."

"What else can she possibly know?" Greg asks.

"Please," I say to Greg. "It's okay. I want to talk to Detective Klein in private." There's only one place this is going and I don't want Mom to hear it.

Greg throws his hands up. "Okay, Abbi, if that's what you want."

Mom agrees to the interview, but she looks worried. Her eyes follow the detective, Officer Delaney, and me as we leave the kitchen. What doesn't she know? What haven't I told her?

In the living room, I sit on the edge of the sofa, and Detective Klein takes a seat in Greg's favorite arm-chair. Officer Delaney sits at the other end of the sofa. She opens a notebook and pulls out a pen, and the detective turns on the recorder and identifies the people in the room again. Then he asks, "Where's your bike?"

He takes me by surprise. What's my bike got to do with anything? It must be a trick question, the kind teachers ask when they already know the answer.

My legs start to itch. At first I think it's just nerves, but then I realize it's poison ivy. I've had it often enough to recognize its horrible, impossible-to-ignore itch. I must have run through a patch of it in the woods.

I'm actually tempted to tell him that my bike was stolen. But he's the detective with the mind-reading eyes. He'll know I'm lying.

"It's at the end of Marie Drive," I whisper. "In some weeds."

"Why did you leave it there?"

My voice drops so low, I have to repeat my answer. "Because Skylar and I followed Jason and Carter into the woods."

"Just to clarify, please state the boys' last names."

"Jason Dobbs and Carter Myers," I say in a small voice. Even though I still don't much like Jason, I hate telling on him.

"Jason Dobbs and Carter Myers," he repeats. "How do you know them?"

"We go to the same middle school. Skylar and I don't have any classes with them, but everybody knows who they are."

Detective Klein nods. "Even I know who they are." He looks at me hard. "It's difficult to imagine you two hanging out with those boys."

"We don't! They were everywhere we went this summer, acting tough and mean."

"So why did you follow them into the woods?" His voice is level, his face blank, but I know he's angry.

"Skylar thought Jason was holding things back, like he probably knew where Ms. Sullivan's phone was." I look at him. "Skylar said we'd get a reward for telling the police. And you'd see we weren't just kids playing detective."

I lean toward him, desperate now. "If I tell you everything that happened in the woods, will you promise not to tell my mother?"

"That's exactly what Skylar asked." Those eyes of his look into mine, and I shut them for a second so he won't see how scared I am.

"This is what I told Skylar," he says. "As long as you girls obey your mothers and stay in the boundaries they've established, I'll keep whatever you tell me to myself. But—if I, or any other police officer, find you somewhere you should not be, the deal is off. Got it?"

"Yes, sir." The rest of the story tumbles out. The trailer, the stripped car, Paul, the drugs, the dog, Ms. Sullivan, the railroad bridge. The whole horrible story— except where Jason is.

I take a deep breath. I feel like I'm choking to death and can barely go on talking. "Jason and Carter saw Paul kill Ms. Sullivan. Paul thought she was after his drugs. So he—so he—"

"Skylar told me the same thing. She believes Jason. Do you?"

"Yes." I look at him. "It wasn't Mr. Boyce after all."

"We never thought it was. We just wanted to ask him a few questions about what happened the day Ms. Sullivan disappeared. If he saw or heard anything, that sort of thing. You know, like they say on those crime shows you love so much."

I'm crying again, and my poison ivy is itching so bad I want to claw the skin off my leg.

Detective Klein leans back in the chair and studies me. "Just what do you think would have happened if Paul had caught you spying on his trailer? You must know what a dangerous man he is."

"If he's so dangerous, why isn't he in jail? Why is he out in the woods selling drugs and stripping cars and killing people?"

I'm still crying, so most of what I say comes out in gulps. The poison ivy is driving me crazy. I've said stuff I wouldn't have if I hadn't been itching so bad.

Detective Klein hands me a tissue and I blow my nose and wipe my eyes, but tears are still dribbling down my cheeks.

He hands me another tissue. "As soon as Skylar told me what Jason said, I sent a team to the trailer to bring Paul in. He's been a suspect from the start. We found Carter there, badly beaten. He's in the hospital being treated for severe dog bites and fractures."

He pauses, steely-eyed again. "So do you have any idea where Jason is?"

I bite my lip hard. "Are you going to arrest him?"

"For what? As far as I know, he hasn't committed a crime. I want to talk to him about what he saw. If he's really an eyewitness, we need him to testify when we bring Paul to trial."

"He's hiding," I say, keeping my eyes away from Detective Klein's stare. "He's really scared Paul will kill him. And he's got a bad cut on his leg that will probably get infected unless he has a tetanus shot."

"If you know where Jason's hiding," Detective Klein says, "you need to tell me. We'll make sure he gets a tetanus shot."

"Paul's really in jail? Not out on bond—or whatever you call it?"

"Don't worry about Paul. We have enough on him to keep him a long time."

"Jason's in the shed in our backyard." I fall back against the sofa and try to breathe normally. I feel like I've been holding my breath since Detective Klein arrived.

He turns to Officer Delaney. "Go get him, but be easy on him. He's just a kid, after all."

I watch her leave. Jason will hate me for sure, but at least he won't get blood poisoning. Someday he just might realize I saved his life, but I'm not counting on it.

Detective Klein gives me another one of his long, mind-searching looks. "You're a smart girl, and so is Skylar, but neither one of you has any sense. Do me a favor and work on acquiring some."

He starts to leave and stops in the doorway. "We picked up your bike. It's at Skylar's house. Oh, and here's your phone."

I press it to my chest like it's a sacred object. My phone, my phone, my dear phone. I'll never let it out of my sight again.

"By the way," he says, "we weren't able to recover your image library. Luckily, we didn't need the pictures."

I look at my phone. Maybe by losing all my pictures, I'm getting off lightly.

Detective Klein goes to the kitchen to have a few more words with Mom and Greg. I hope he won't tell her about Paul and the trailer. I could be wrong, but he seems like the kind of person who keeps his word.

While they're talking, I look out the front window and see Jason limping toward the police car with Officer Delaney. She has one hand on his shoulder. He doesn't look at my house or Skylar's house. With his head down, he climbs into the back seat of the police car. Detective Klein says goodbye to me, goes outside, and gets into the car beside Officer Delaney. Jason doesn't even glance out the window as they leave.

I take a deep breath. Mom did not see Jason get into the police car. If she had, she'd ask me who he was and what he was doing in our shed and I would have had to spin some crazy explanation that she wouldn't have believed and before I could stop myself, I'd be telling her about the nightmare in the woods. She'd probably send me to a convent school in Switzerland.

It's almost nine o'clock, not quite dark. The night cicadas are singing in the trees and I am so tired I can hardly stand up.

I ask Mom and Greg if I can go to bed. I haven't heard the end of this, not by a long shot, but at least they let me leave the kitchen without another lecture.

In the bathroom, I slather my legs with calamine lotion. The itch almost goes away, but I know it will be back. If I hadn't been running for my life, I would have noticed the poison ivy, but when you're terrified of one huge thing, you don't think about little ordinary things.

I get into bed and check the messages on my phone. No new ones, not even from Skylar. I think maybe I should text her and ask how things went at her house, but then I remember that she dropped her phone in the water. I'm so tired. Too much has happened today. I can't make sense of any of it. I want to sleep for a hundred years and wake up with no memory.

I'll see Skylar tomorrow. We'll talk then.

13

The next morning, Mom and I watch the news while we eat breakfast. So far, she hasn't had much to say. The silent treatment is her way of telling me she's mad. And disappointed. I've gone way beyond the limits this time.

A solemn-faced anchorman appears on the screen. "Police have charged Paul Blake, a local drug dealer, with the murder of Kristina Sullivan, a popular teacher at Everett Stone Middle School. He was taken into custody last night and charged with murder in the first degree, assault, operating a meth lab, drug trafficking, car theft, and a host of lesser offenses."

A picture of Ms. Sullivan appears briefly on the screen, followed by a clip of Paul being pulled out of a police car, his head down, his hands cuffed behind his back.

"Isn't that the man Greg knows?" Mom asks. "The one we saw at the DQ?"

"It looks like him." I'm trying not to scratch my poison ivy. If Mom sees it, she'll ask me where I got it.

"More details tonight," the newsman promises. Mom clicks the remote and the screen goes blank.

I scratch while Mom's not looking, but she notices anyway. Eyes in the back of her head, as they say.

"Is that poison ivy?"

"I guess so." I stare at the ugly, oozing rash as if I'd never seen it before. "I don't know how I got it. I'm so careful."

"Somewhere around that tree house, most likely." She takes our dishes to the sink and manages to make a lot of disapproving noises by turning the water on full blast and spraying plates, cups, and glasses like she's pressure washing them.

I know what she's thinking: *Serves you right. If you'd stayed where you belong, you would not have poison ivy.*

I start to leave, but before I'm half out of my chair, she says, "Sit down. I have something to say to you."

Uh-oh. Here it comes. I sit down and brace myself. She stands at the sink with a plate in her hand.

"Greg and I were talking after you went to bed last night. We decided it might be a good idea if you didn't see Skylar for a while."

I don't expect this. "Skylar's my best friend. She lives right across the street. You can't keep us apart."

"Will you please stop scratching?" Mom yells like she's suddenly gone nuts. "You're making the poison ivy worse! Do you want it to spread all over you? Go soak in salt water. Then smear calamine lotion on your legs." She tosses a box of salt to me and starts throwing plates into the dishwasher.

I run upstairs, crying, turn on the hot water, and dump the whole box of salt into the tub. Then I get in. The water's almost scalding, but my legs stop itching.

I lie in the tub and look at the ceiling. What will I do without Skylar? We've been friends since I moved here in third grade. We're the super-duper dynamic duo, inseparable. We're two halves of an apple. *Essere l'altra metà della mela.* The Italian words are so beautiful I memorized them, but I can't say them the way Greg did.

I stay in the tub so long the water turns cold. The tips of my fingers get wrinkles and I begin to itch again. Finally I heave myself out and get dressed. I slather my legs with so much calamine lotion it cracks like pink mud as it dries. The smell is like summer.

I'm not ready to face Mom, so I lie on my bed and finish reading *Fahrenheit 451*. I watched the movie with Greg before I read the book, and I remember the ending, where people walk around reciting books in soft voices. Ray Bradbury's ending is very different. The hero of the story meets up with a group of men who memorize books, but there's no peaceful community, no women, no children. The United States has destroyed itself in a terrible war, and the men are alone, hoping to contact other readers and start a better world. I like the movie's ending better, but probably Bradbury's ending is more realistic—except there should be a few women in the group.

For my fifth and final book I choose *To Kill a Mockingbird*. I have my own well-read copy. I know what happens and how it ends. It's sometimes sad, sometimes funny, and sometimes scary, but that's just the kind of story I need now, especially one that has no surprises for me. No sudden and horrible twists of fate. No dead animals—well, except for the rabid dog Atticus shoots. The death of a rabid dog is okay. You can die from rabies.

The Red Pony pops into my head, and I imagine how Steinbeck would write that scene. First of all, the dog would be Jem's beloved pet. When the dog gets rabies, Atticus would make Jem shoot his very own pet. I'm glad Harper Lee didn't write the story like that.

To keep Skylar and me apart, Mom makes sure that I spend the weekend with her and Greg. On Saturday afternoon we go to Greenbrier Lake. Greg rents a canoe, something Mom can't afford, but it just makes me feel hot and sick and itchy. On Sunday we go to Harpers Ferry. It takes forever to get there. We walk around the town, up and down steep hills, with crowds of people and crying kids all pushing and jostling and talking so loud my ears hurt. After lunch, which I can't eat, we cross a bridge over the Potomac River and watch rock climbers scramble up a steep rock face. Then we walk at least a hundred miles on the canal towpath.

It's more like a punishment than a fun weekend. My poison ivy itches and itches and itches. The hot sun makes it worse. I still feel nauseated from swallowing the water in the Paint Branch—although it might just be psychological and have nothing to do with the water in the stream.

I miss Skylar. On a normal day, she'd be with us. We'd be laughing, having fun, acting silly. Greg would tease us. Mom would be in a good mood. Maybe we'd stop for dinner and Skylar and I would have giggle fits about something.

We come home after dark. Skylar's bedroom light is off. I wonder what she's been doing all day. Does she feel bad about not being invited to come with us? Did she get a new phone? I think about texting her before

I go to bed, but I'm just too tired to pick up my phone. I'll talk to her tomorrow.

Monday is the first day of being grounded. Skylar and I haven't talked for two days. She hasn't texted me, and I haven't texted her. Now we're sitting side by side on her porch steps.

"Where were you all weekend?" she asks me.

"Oh," I say in a dull voice. "Greg and Mom dragged me to Greenbrier Lake on Saturday and then to Harpers Ferry on Sunday. It was hot and crowded and totally boring."

"How come you didn't take me?"

I try to come up with a reason that isn't the real reason. "They wanted to do a family thing, just the three of us."

Skylar looks at me. "Your mom blames me for what we did. She doesn't want you hanging out with me. I'm a bad influence, right?"

I shake my head. "She's mad at me, not you."

Skylar gives me her slit-eyed stare. "You never could tell a lie, Abbi. Admit it. Your mom has never liked me all that much."

My poison ivy starts itching and it's all I can do not to scratch it. I don't want to have this talk. I'd rather go home and read or something, but before I can leave,

Rob sits down with us. He's been mowing the grass and he's so sweaty his skin shines.

My heart speeds up, skips around. I look down to hide the blush heating my face. No matter what Skylar thinks of her brother, I still have a secret crush on him. I don't even dare to say hi because I might give myself away, and Skylar will guess and never stop teasing me.

"Abs," he says to me, "I hear you and Sky just can't stay away from Marie Drive—hanging out in a tree house with Jason and Carter, spying on people, riding your bikes all over town. You even told the cops Mr. Boyce killed Ms. Sullivan. It's juvenile detention for sure."

I look at Skylar. "Did you tell him?"

Rob answers before Skylar gets a word out. "I heard the interview. After that detective left, Mom screamed at Skylar all night. Your mom must have gone nuts too."

Skylar looks like she's about to punch Rob. "Shut up, pothead."

"Get over it, Sky. Buying that stuff was a once-in-a-lifetime mistake."

"Once in a lifetime?" she says. "Don't make me laugh."

Rob goes inside and the storm door slams behind him.

Suddenly I don't want to be here anymore. Skylar is in a terrible mood. I hate the way she talks to Rob. It's hot, there's nothing to do except play Spit or Hearts or some other dumb card game, and my legs are itching like crazy.

I tell Skylar I'm going home. "I need more calamine."

Skylar looks at my legs, now caked with a thick pink layer of cracked lotion. You can see oozing blisters underneath. Not a pretty sight.

"Boy, am I glad I don't get that stuff," she says. "Your legs look like something in a horror movie. A zombie maybe, with its skin falling off."

Skylar has never, ever said anything like this to me. To Rob maybe, but not to me. My feelings are really hurt. "Well, don't look at them, then."

I walk away. I expect Skylar to come after me and apologize, but she doesn't.

Rob catches up with me. He has my bike. "The detective left this in our yard."

I take it without looking at him because I'm crying again.

"Hey, Abs, don't cry. You know how Sky is—she's mad for a few days and then she's over it."

"I don't even know why she's mad."

"Neither do I. You know what? I don't think she knows either. Things upset her, that's all. Give her time. That's what Mom and I do."

He jogs away. His legs are straight and muscled, just like Skylar's. The sun lights his hair, making it blonder. He glances over his shoulder, grins, and waves. Then he turns the corner and disappears behind Mr. Schuman's hedge.

I hope Rob's right. I know why Skylar's mad at him, but I don't know what I did to offend her. Maybe she's mad at the whole world and taking it out on me.

I walk my bike into the garage. The tires are flat, the wheels are muddy, and weeds are tangled in the spokes. I'll never ride it again. Maybe I should put it on the curb for the garbage collectors.

Just as Rob predicted, Skylar gets over being mad the next day. She even apologizes for what she said about my poison ivy. Zombie legs become something to laugh about. I threaten to rub my legs against hers so she'll be a zombie too.

When I try to talk about what happened in the woods, Skylar says, "I'm done with that. It happened, it's over. We should've spent the summer at the pool. That tree house was a dumb kid idea."

I need to understand why it happened, what we did, how she feels about it, but she's locking her memories in a secret Skylar room. Done. Over. Finished. Maybe she thinks the whole thing will shrink into the past, like something that happened long ago when we were too young to know better.

I'd like to be done with it, too, only what happened to us is always with me like an itch under my skin that I can't scratch. I live it over and over in nightmares. Even when I'm awake, I see flashes of Ms. Sullivan running into the woods and Mr. Boyce sitting in the SUV, doing nothing to stop her. I smell the dead deer and the polluted water of the Paint Branch. I'm terrified Paul will get out of jail and kill Skylar and me.

If only we could go back to the way we were before— two halves of the same apple, sharing everything, no secrets.

Skylar's new phone beeps. She picks it up and starts texting.

"Who's that?" I lean toward her to see but she moves away, shielding the phone.

I shrug like she hasn't hurt my feelings and turn to my phone. I can't think of anyone to text, so I scroll through my email, which doesn't take much time. Skylar is so rude.

Finally, she stops texting and turns to me with a big grin. "That was Jonathon. He got my number from Erica. He asked me why I haven't been at the pool. He misses me."

"What did you tell him?"

"That I was tired of the pool. I wasn't about to tell him I'm grounded."

She jumps up from the porch steps and does a little dance. "I think he really, truly, definitely likes me!"

I guess I'm supposed to congratulate her, but I just sit there. A cat crosses the yard, the neighbor's dog barks at it. Someone starts a lawn mower. Skylar and me, a hot summer day, Ms. Freeman in the kitchen talking on the phone. On the surface everything's the same as always, year after year, the two of us sitting on these steps asking each other what we want to do today.

I turn to Skylar, but she's texting again—Erica this time. I feel left out and make up an excuse to go home. She waves goodbye without looking at me.

A few days later, our mothers agree we can go to the mall. Ms. Freeman drives. It's the first thing we've done together since we were grounded. Instead of riding in the back seat with me, Skylar sits beside her mother and I get into the back by myself. Skylar checks messages on her phone, and I watch houses and apartment buildings and stores drift past. I feel like texting her and saying, *Hey, I'm sitting behind you.*

We meet Nessa, Erica, and Lindsey at the food court. For the first time ever, Skylar talks to Erica instead of me. From the way they whisper, it seems they have some private stuff going on. They giggle a lot. Skylar says in a loud voice, "I did not say that!" They laugh so hard Erica knocks her soda over.

Soon Jonathon and his friends show up. He sits next to Skylar, so close their shoulders touch. It's like no one exists for her except him. He whispers in her ear. She blushes and pushes him away. He laughs and kisses her cheek. She pretends to be mad, but I can tell she's faking.

Lindsey giggles and nudges me. "They're in love," she whispers.

"You must know all about it," Nessa says.

I smile and nod like it's a secret I can't tell, but Skylar hasn't told me anything about Jonathon since the day he texted her.

After the boys leave for endless soccer practice, I end up hanging out with Lindsey and Nessa while Skylar and Erica continue their private talk. Nessa asks me if I know Mr. Boyce has been fired.

I shake my head, kind of stunned. "How do you know?"

"Our neighbor, Mrs. Barker, works at the school office," Nessa says. "She typed the letter the principal sent him. It was because of his relationship with Ms. Sullivan. His wife left him, too."

"Erica always said he was getting a divorce," Lindsey adds.

Skylar hears us and leans across the table. "He sure got what he deserved."

Nessa frowns. "I think it's sad what happened to him. He was the best teacher I ever had. Don't you remember how much we loved him? And little Andy?"

"I feel sorry for little Andy," Skylar says, "but not him."

"What do you all think?" Nessa looks at each of us.

"I'm with Skylar," Erica says. "We both know plenty about divorce and cheating dads and all that stuff."

Lindsey looks embarrassed. "I don't want to talk about it. It's horrible. I loved him and Ms. Sullivan both and now she's dead and it's partly his fault."

"She knew he was married, though," Erica mutters in such a low voice that I'm not even sure she really said it.

Nessa looks at me. "How about you, Abbi?"

"I'm kind of like you. I know it was wrong of him, but I feel sort of sorry for him anyway. But I feel a lot more sorry for Ms. Sullivan." Pictures of her flash through my head. I think of the paintings she would never paint, the books she'd never read, the places she'd never go. I bite my lip and will myself not to cry.

Skylar pushes her chair back and gets to her feet. "The Gap's having a big back-to-school sale. Let's go."

We all get up and move toward the Gap. Nessa and I lag behind the others. "You look upset, Abbi," she says.

"It's just so sad." I wipe my eyes with the back of my hand and sniffle. "I liked them both so much."

"Me, too." Nessa sighs. "Mr. Boyce just wasn't as great as we thought."

Like that saying about idols with clay feet, I think.

We catch up with the others in the Gap. Erica's holding up a blue T-shirt. "Let's all get one of these and wear it on the first day of school."

I worry we'll look like a gang, but since everybody else likes the idea, I go along with them. Even though the shirt is 20 percent off, I spend almost every cent of the shopping money Mom gave me. Skylar comes up short, and Erica lends her five dollars.

We leave the Gap and meet Ms. Freeman in the parking lot. Skylar gets in the front seat; I get in the back. I guess this is the way things are now.

With a week of summer vacation left, Skylar and I are sitting on her porch steps.

"Did you see the announcement for Ms. Sullivan's memorial service?" I ask her. "It was in yesterday's *Flier*."

"I never read the *Flier*. It's boring." She looks up from her phone. "When is it?"

"This Sunday at the Nature Conservancy. Do you want to go together? We can ride with Mom and Greg in the truck."

"Do you think Mr. Boyce will be there?"

"Probably not."

"If I was him," Skylar says, "I wouldn't be caught dead at the memorial."

We look at each other, not sure whether to laugh at "be caught dead" or pretend Skylar didn't say it.

"I didn't say *dead* on purpose," she says. "It just slipped out."

We laugh a little, more of a nervous giggle than a real laugh.

I wind a twist of hair around my finger. It's down to my shoulders now but still looking wispy. "What should we do if he does show up?"

Skylar frowns. "What do you mean?"

"Should we say hi and talk to him or what?"

She shakes her head. "I'm not saying *anything* to him. If I see him, I'll look the other way."

"But, Skylar—"

"Look, Abbi, I'm sorry he got fired, but I don't want to talk to him."

My poison ivy is almost gone, but if I sit here in the hot sun arguing with Skylar, it's bound to start itching again. "Okay," I say. "Okay, but even if you don't, I feel sad for him. Maybe we shouldn't have gone to the police. Maybe we just made things worse for him. He didn't kill her."

Skylar stares at me. "What he did was *wrong*, Abbi. He had a wife and a baby. He was a cheater. He ruined Andy's life. You know how I feel about that." She turns away. "I gotta go. Mom's going out, and I promised to fix dinner for the pothead and me."

Skylar runs into her house. The door shuts with a bang behind her. I want to run after her and shout, *Why are you always mad at me? What did I do that you didn't do? You've been my best friend since third grade and I can't even talk to you!*

Instead, I stand on the porch and wait for the door to open and Skylar to come out and say she's sorry and why don't I stay for dinner or something.

The door doesn't open. Skylar doesn't come out.

I walk home and finish reading *To Kill a Mockingbird*. Why didn't I get a father like Atticus? Why didn't Skylar?

Does anybody really have a father like Atticus? Or a brother like Jem?

14

The Saturday before the memorial for Ms. Sullivan, Mom takes me to the mall to shop for something to wear. Something *suitable,* she says. All I have are shorts and jeans and T-shirts. Nobody wears dresses or skirts now, I tell her. But Mom doesn't believe me. Off we go.

It's embarrassing to be at the mall with my mother, especially on a Saturday. That's the day kids go with their friends. You get teased if you're seen with your mother. It's like you don't have any friends to go with. Which makes it worse because right now I'm scared that I don't have any friends. Maybe Nessa and Erica and Lindsey don't really like me. They just put up with me when I'm with Skylar. Without her, I'm a nothing.

I don't know how to explain this to Mom. It's not like I hate her the way some girls hate their mothers. It's just the way it is. You don't go to the mall or the movies or the pool with your mother unless you're under eleven.

We enter the mall through Macy's. "Let's start here," Mom says.

Even though I'm sure I won't find anything I like, I go along with her suggestion. My friends don't shop here.

She stops at the jewelry counter to look at earrings. "All the ones I like best are for pierced ears," she says.

"You could get your ears pierced," I say, but she's moving on to the shoe department. She picks up a sandal here and a running shoe there. She fingers lipsticks at a cosmetics counter and lingers in the purse department.

"We came here to find something for me," I remind her. "Teen clothes are on the other side of the store."

In the teen department, Mom begins searching through racks of hideous clothes. She holds up a dress. "Oh, look, Abbi, this is adorable."

I shake my head. "Please, Mom, just let me wear jeans and my new blue T-shirt," I beg. To be honest, I don't want to buy something to wear at Ms. Sullivan's memorial. I'll never see it without remembering why I own it.

"Let's try another store." Before I can stop her, Mom walks out of Macy's and heads straight for the

Gap. She might as well be Skylar, the way she bosses me around.

I walk several steps behind Mom and pause at the entrance to the Gap to take a quick look at the shoppers inside. No one I know is there. Ignoring the blouse Mom's waving like a flag, I find a rack of skirts and paw through them. I see a skirt with small white flowers on a black background that looks okay and grab one in my size. I snatch a black T-shirt too and show them to Mom.

"Perfect," she says. "Did you try them on?"

"Yes," I lie, and lead her toward the cashiers.

There's a line, of course. While we're waiting, Nessa appears with her mother. She runs over to see what I have, asks where I found it, and picks out something similar. Her mother is holding up a barf green sweater. Nessa is just as embarrassed as I'd be.

Next stop is Brown's Shoe Store, where I find a pair of black sandals, little strappy things, and Mom buys them for me. Then it's on to lunch. Luckily she heads for the café in Nordstrom's. It's a mom place. My friends will definitely not be eating there.

We order sandwiches and choose a quiet booth in the back of the café. While we're eating, Mom asks if Skylar wants to ride to the memorial with us.

"She isn't going."

Mom looks surprised. "Why not?"

"She doesn't want to see Mr. Boyce."

"I don't think he'll be there," Mom says. "Not after what happened."

"He might be." I pull the fancy toothpick out of my sandwich and twirl it in my fingers.

"Are you worried about seeing him?"

I snap the toothpick in half. "Kind of."

"Because you and Skylar reported him to the police?"

I nod, too ashamed to look up. "We shouldn't have done it. Skylar feels bad too, but she won't admit it. I think it's messing up our friendship."

She puts her finger under my chin and lifts my head so I have to look at her. "I wish you'd talked to me before you went to the police, but you had reasons to distrust Mr. Boyce, even to suspect him of murdering Ms. Sullivan. The police had no way of knowing about the relationship or that he was the last person to see her alive. You and Skylar didn't act out of malice. You thought you were doing the right thing."

I poke at the mound of uneaten french fries on my plate. "You don't think I ruined his life?"

Mom squeezes my hand. "Of course not. I'm pretty sure Mr. Boyce doesn't blame you and Skylar for what happened. He knew it was wrong to get into a relationship with Ms. Sullivan. As an adult, he has to take responsibility for his behavior."

I listen to what she says, but I still feel bad about what Skylar and I did. Maybe Mr. Boyce wasn't who we thought he was, but how did we convince ourselves he could murder anyone? Even Jason, who never had Mr. Boyce for a teacher, laughed at us for thinking he was a killer.

Mom squeezes my hand again. "Mr. Boyce made some big mistakes. You and Skylar made some big mistakes too. Unfortunately, you can't go back in time and change anything. You just have to live with it."

"When you found out what I did, I was scared you hated me. I thought you might even find my father and give me to him."

Mom laughs. "Never, never, never. Not in a million years. I don't know where your father is, and I don't care."

"I wish Greg was my father," I blurt. "If you married him, he would be."

"Oh, Abbi, I love Greg. Maybe I'll marry him, maybe I won't. He's a great guy, but marriage is a huge commitment."

Maybe, maybe, I think. At least she didn't say *never in a million years.*

"You and Ms. Freeman," I say. "She doesn't want to get married either."

"Nikki has lots of issues from her first marriage," Mom says.

"So does Skylar. One reason she doesn't want to see Mr. Boyce is because he cheated on his wife, just like her dad. I don't think she'll ever stop being mad at her father."

Mom sighs. "Nikki is very bitter. I told her once that she should consider family counseling, but that made her so mad I thought our friendship was over."

"Skylar must be more like her mom than she thinks."

Mom laughs. "It sounds like it."

After lunch, Mom and I pass a jewelry store advertising ear piercing.

"'Done by a certified nurse under sterile conditions,'" Mom reads. "I've always wanted pierced ears. How about you? Your friend in the Gap had the cutest little hoops in her ears. What do you say? A mother-daughter memory!"

I'm almost too amazed to say anything. Skylar and I have often talked about getting our ears pierced, but we were sure our mothers would say no. Now here is my mother, so much more uptight than Ms. Freeman, offering me the chance.

"Yes," I say. "Yes!"

We leave the mall with little silver studs in our ears. We plan to get matching hoops in a couple of weeks.

It's the best day we've had together for a long time.

15

On Sunday afternoon Mom and Greg and I go to the memorial service. It's one of the few days in August when the air is cool and the humidity low. In some places, this would be a sign that fall's coming, but here in Maryland I know hot weather is around the next corner, waiting to jump out and send the temperature roaring into the nineties again.

At the Nature Conservancy, Greg drives up a long, straight graveled road. He looks at the fields stretching out on either side of us. Groves of trees, an old barn, picnic tables in the shade.

"What a pretty place," he says. "I've never noticed it before. Never even heard of it. Do people get married here?"

He laughs like it's a joke, but from the back seat I see Mom's ears turn red. I hold the idea close and cross my fingers.

"Ms. Sullivan loved the conservancy," I tell Greg. "She brought our art class here last spring. We sat outside and drew. *Plein air*, it's called. She set up her easel and painted the old barn and the field and the hay bales. She was such a good artist."

A lump swells in my throat, and I turn my head. I don't want to cry. But I miss her so much.

I miss Skylar too. She should be sitting in the little back seat with me, bumping knees and elbows, sharing everything, even the sad times like this. *Essere l'altra metà della mela.*

Greg parks his truck in an overflow area on the grass, and we walk toward the crowd of people gathered on a hilltop. I look at the barn and remember Ms. Sullivan standing at her easel, talking to us while she painted. I take Mom's hand.

I see Nessa and Lindsey with their parents. Nessa's wearing the skirt she bought at the Gap, and Lindsey has on a dress that makes her look older than Nessa. I wave and they wave back. Erica stands a little apart from her mother, talking to Jonathon's friend David.

Mom and Greg and I walk around the grounds—like a family, I think. We stop and talk to some of my teachers. I say hello to kids I know, but all of us stay close to our parents, as if we're in danger.

Before the service begins, I go to the ladies' room.

When I come out, I almost bump into Mr. Boyce.

My heart leaps in my chest and thunders. Blood rushes to my face. I can barely look at him. He can't be happy to see me.

"Abbi," he says. "Where's your other half?"

"Skylar couldn't come, she had to do something else, I don't remember what . . ." My voice sort of flutters away, and I clear my throat.

"You look very nice," Mr. Boyce says. "Grown up, almost."

I touch one of my earrings. "Mom let me get my ears pierced," I tell him. "I can wear bigger ones in a couple of weeks, you know, after my ears heal."

I blush again—why am I talking about earrings? What is wrong with me? Shouldn't I be telling him I'm sorry I spied on him and Ms. Sullivan, sorry I told the police, sorry I thought you killed Ms. Sullivan, sorry you lost your job and your wife left you. Even though I know these things are not my fault, I'm still so sorry, so very sorry, but I just can't force the words out of my mouth. It's like they're too big to say.

Mr. Boyce smiles. At least his mouth does. His hair is combed, his face shaved. He's wearing a navy blue jacket, a pale blue shirt, and khaki pants, a typical Mr. Boyce outfit. He seems older somehow, and his eyes are still sad.

I try to smile back, but I'm thinking how nice he's

being when he must totally hate me. I should tell him I'm sorry, but it's hard to talk because of the huge lump in my throat.

"I almost didn't come today," he says. "But Kris meant so much to me. I wanted to be here for her. Even if . . ."

His voice breaks. "I know what people think, what they say—if I'd gone after her that day, she'd still be alive." His eyes linger on the meadows running downhill to the woods. "I'll always blame myself for her death, for letting her go, for not stopping her."

I squint up at him. The sun's in my eyes and my sandal straps are rubbing my heels. I'm embarrassed. I don't know what to say. I hadn't expected Mr. Boyce to tell me how he felt, as if I were another grown up, not a kid. Sweat trickles down my sides.

"I should go. Mom will wonder where I am." I stumble over the words like I'm giving a speech I didn't prepare for. Before I lose my nerve, I add, "I'm sorry about the police and all. Skylar and I, we . . . well, we—"

"Don't worry about it, Abbi. I'm sorry too. I handled everything so badly."

A teacher, Ms. Russell, comes out of the restroom. Without even looking at Mr. Boyce, she says, "The memorial starts in five minutes, Abbi."

Mr. Boyce pretends not to notice the snub. "It's nice to see you, Abbi. Enjoy eighth grade. Keep pulling down those As, you and Skylar both. And don't worry—you two will always be my one and only super-duper dynamic duo."

I hurry away, then stop and look back. "It was good to see you too, Mr. Boyce."

He's already deep in a conversation with Mr. Ignazio, the eighth-grade science teacher. But he raises a hand to wave.

I walk slowly uphill to Mom and Greg, the sun beating down on me, sweat trickling down my back. I feel better about Mr. Boyce, but it would have been nice if Skylar had been with me. We could talk about what he told me. Surely she'd be glad to see how sorry he is. Maybe she'd even forgive him, at least a little.

I stand between Mom and Greg, holding hands with both of them. I see Mr. Boyce at the back of the crowd. He's by himself.

After a pair of folk singers play a couple of sad songs, the principal gives a talk in praise of Ms. Sullivan and reads a poem by Robert Frost. Teachers, friends, and relatives step forward and share their memories—long hikes in the mountains, bike rides, visits to the ocean, art galleries and museums, train rides to New York. Her family talks about her childhood and how she'd always wanted to be an artist. They laugh about her sense of humor and cry about how much they miss her.

Behind the speakers is a display of Ms. Sullivan's

artwork. Among the pictures is the barn I saw her paint. It's so beautiful. I wish it hung on my bedroom wall where I could see it every day.

At the end, we all hold hands and sing "Will the Circle Be Unbroken," one of Ms. Sullivan's favorite songs. Everybody cries. I glimpse Mr. Boyce walking away alone, his head down.

On the way to the truck, Greg hugs me. "What a nice way to remember your teacher."

"It was beautiful," I say.

"Perfect," Mom adds.

We walk together, me in the middle, holding hands again. I think of Mr. Boyce getting into his car and driving away from Evansburg. I think of Ms. Sullivan standing at an easel painting that barn. I think of Skylar and me and the strange distance that's opened between us. I touch the silver studs in my ears and wonder what eighth grade will be like.

MORE THRILLING STORIES FROM
MARY DOWNING HAHN!

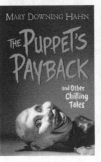